Harlot's grace

L.M. Pampuro

L.M. Pampuro

Harlot's grace

L.M. Pampuro

Harlot's grace
Copyright 2019 by L.M. Pampuro

This book is a work of fiction.
Names, characters, locations, and events are either a product of the author's imagination, fictitious or used fictitiously.

Any resemblance to any event, locale or person, living or dead, is purely coincidental.

Cover design by the LMPatarini group

ISBN: 978-1-7344990-1-8

To the dreamers...
Peace.

L.M. Pampuro

Although only a few ounces, the small round piece of gold weighed twenty pounds in her hand. Alia held it out, closer to him than her as her hand refused to bring the offensive sight near her body.

"I am not going to ask again." His voice is unruffled. No emotion. At this point, why should there be?

"I have a condition—"

"Whatever it is, we can work it out." Alia leaned forward in her chair.

"Actually, it is more like a disease..."

"A disease, you say?" He raised one eyebrow. A gesture she used to love yet now loathe. "Does this disease have a name?"

"Yes. It is called Wanderlust." His laugh caught the attention of others in the restaurant. The silence grew as other patrons glanced in their direction.

"Wanderlust, you say?" He shook his head no, still with a smile. "Are you sure it isn't A. T. M. J.?" She ran the letters through my brain. ATMJ? WTF? "Addicted to my job?" Alia shook her head no, although getting married would complicate her position more than just casual dating.

Across the table, her companion stared at his fingernails. He was pleasant enough, definitely attractive if one is into that hot middle management guy in a suit type. Of course, Salvi Giovani was no middle management. His eyes begged while the rest sat back in the wooden chair, lips curved upward.

He did have self-confidence; she would give him that. "My job," or at least the one he thought she had, "has nothing to do with this. What is wrong with the status quo?" *Shit!* She did it again.

He lifted the weight from her palm, and a loud swoosh escaped from her mouth. "I guess this is it." He rose to leave.

Alia sat there. She sat and let this possibly exceptional human walk out of her life. He moved in a straight path for the door. He didn't glance back.

While she ping-ponged between sadness and relief, the waiter slipped a bill in front of her for fifty bucks. "For the drinks."

She pulled a c-note from her pocket and laid it on the plastic holder. "Just keep it," she followed the same worn carpet out the door. The only difference, she glimpsed back.

"Alia, you made the right decision," Alister Otis Reed brought his hand down on his massive, oak desk. "Think about the complications this could cause for our mission." Alister believed that the only successful marriages were agent to agent, and even those ended in divorce 65% of the time. The number skyrocketed after retirement.

"Why do I feel so…" His young agent's voice trailed off.

L.M. Pampuro

"That will go away," he flipped his hand in the air to swat away all her emotion. "I am proud of you."

Alister's last words echoed. Alia knew that she didn't belong with Salvi Giovani forever. His presence kept both families off their back as far as expectations of getting older, producing grandkids, and getting married. In her eyes, Salvi was a good guy. He worked hard at the Matteo Corporation, the family business his grandfather founded back in the 1930s.

Grandpa began bootlegging hooch in New Britain, Connecticut. His brother delivered the loaded trucks of their contraband all over New England and upstate New York during prohibition. A soda bottler in town washed the glass and, on occasion, allowed the Giovani brothers to use his equipment to speed up the bottling process.

After booze became legal again, so did their operation. Grandpa named the legitimate company, The Matteo Corporation, after his first-born male grandson. Her Salvi is the second grandchild, sandwiched between the great Matteo and a princess, spoiled younger sister. Not that any of the Giovani kids suffered. Salvi knew he would never take over as C.E.O. nor would he ever rise to family favorite. For now, he pretends in middle management to be in charge of marketing, a job he loathes.

Alister had checked out the Giovani family operations when Alia began to date Salvi. He proclaimed the family to be clean, although he asked that she didn't reveal her real job. "Do this for me," Alister had requested.

Alia became a writer for "*a small magazine that you wouldn't have heard of*," at least that was her standard line when asked what she did for a living. She enjoyed Salvi's company yet couldn't see herself with him long term. His habit of regularly clearing his throat would eventually put her over the edge.

"Alia," her name brought her back to the present, "now that your pending nuptials are off the table, can we talk about our latest problem?" Alia motioned for Alister to continue, "I brought Johnny DeLuca back to help out with the case."

"Johnny, why?" As if Alia didn't have enough troubles, now Johnny DeLuca. She folded her arms under her breasts. Her blank expression met Alister's gaze.

"Because at one time he was a good agent. He is familiar with the area. Alia, we need his ear on the street. There were four more overdoses last night."

"In Hartford again?"

"Not this time," Alister took a dramatic pause, "Two in West Hartford, two east of the river. This, in addition to both Middlesex and New Britain General adding ten psych patients each who have similar pre-symptoms to those who have passed."

"Holy—"

"Language, Alia!"

"—crap!"

"Indeed. We have a line on a few of the distributors, yet I have instructed not to bring anyone in until we have charges that will stick. Rumors confirm there are too many slick lawyers on their payroll. I want every single one to rot in jail." A red glow crept on to Alister's face. His right fingers gripped his pen so hard, and the skin turned white. Alia waited for a burst of plastic and ink.

Alister pushed a button on his desk. The 60" flat screen on the wall behind him brightened. Alia studied the map of Central Connecticut covered in red and blue dots.

"The red dots indicate where those persons currently residing in psychiatric, and where those who are dead were found. The blue dots indicate where we have busted distributors."

Alia brought her attention to the concentration of blue in Hartford. Alister widened the view to include New Haven along with a small cluster in New London county. "Where is that?" Alia pointed to the area east of the Connecticut River.

"Lyme," he said. "We have one distributor who lives up in these hills."

"Isn't that in the middle of nowhere?"

"Everywhere is somewhere," Alister answered. "The property is outside the Nehantic State Forest. It shares an entryway. There are four houses on the street. The further in, the more expensive and expansive the houses become. Our guy lives in the first house, a modular that resembles a double-wide. As far as we can see, he lives alone. His property is nothing fancy yet well-kept."

"Who else is on the street?"

Alister pushed a folder across this desk. "Take a read. Talk to Johnny." Alia opened her mouth to protest, "I see that you two are not the best of friends, but you have to work together. No discussion." She shut her mouth. "Check in with me after you meet."

Alia rose to leave. *Johnny DeLuca, God, help me.*

Alia arrived at Mozzicato's Café in Hartford's south end at precisely eleven, the agreed-upon time for her meeting with Johnny DeLuca.

Of course, he wasn't there.

She studied the narrow aisle, pastry case, and coffee bar on her right—a row of booths down the left. The last box guarded the restrooms and sported the gold *Reserved* sign. The owners tended to do this for neighborhood V.I.P. s and the local politicians.

Alia took seat three-quarters of the way down in one of the booths. She faced the entrance. All around people spoke in Italian or broken English mixed with Italian. The buzz of the espresso machine combined with the clanking of cups and saucers filled in any pause in the conversation.

She ordered an American coffee with cream and sugar along with a small flaky pastry stuffed with almond paste. She couldn't pronounce the name, "that one." Alia smiled politely as other patrons passed, acknowledged her with a nod, and a mutter *"non appartiene."* Alia didn't understand much Italian, yet the smirks told her she should not be taking up space in this café.

Thirty minutes and two cups of coffee later, the door swung open, and a giant glow entered. Each patron greeted Johnny by name. He shook hands and gave hugs like a politician as he slid down the aisle right passed Alia. He said something in perfect Italian that made the waitress laugh.

Alia waited for a beat before she turned to see Johnny in the back booth. He grinned at her and raised the small espresso cup engulfed by his giant hand. Alia turned her focus back to the exit. Her foot bounced. The caffeine kicked in. Her arms automatically went across her under her breasts. She pictured a line of steam extending out from her ears.

Above the front register, the small clock's ticks echoed against the paneled walls. Alia turned around to see Johnny, grin now gone. His arms rested across his massive chest. "I can do this all day," he said without any motion.

Alia turned back to the front. She concentrated on the speckled ceiling, mumbled "asshole." Several older women dressed head to toe in black in line at the pastry counter turned to give the death stare. One made a tsk noise, the other tilted her head in the direction of her booth.

Alia grabbed her bag, threw a twenty on the table, and as graceful as she could, slid out of the booth to stomp towards Johnny. "You didn't see me sitting there?" she spoke at the same time she slipped in the space across. Johnny filled her view along with a wood panel wall with an old photo of a piazza in Florence above his head.

The photo had a rip in the lower-left corner.

L.M. Pampuro

"I saw you," Johnny said. "I like this booth better."

"I thought this was Victor's booth. There was a reserved sign here." Alia answered.

"You did your homework."

"No, I practically lived in this part of the city for a while." Johnny didn't reply. The waitress came by with another espresso for Johnny. She placed a cup of American coffee in front of Alia. Johnny stared at her mug and grinned.

"I guess you know the neighborhood. Why do you need me?"

"I don't," she glanced behind her, "but Alister thinks we do, so I am here. Where's Lucy?"

"Working." Johnny drank the espresso in a single shot. "Alister gave me some background. We are looking for drug dealers?"

"More than the distributors. We have information that the junk might be manufactured close by too." Alia turned her entire body around to scan the room. She pushed back on the bench to now rest against the wall. With a turn of the head and angles of the mirrors behind the counter, she could survey the room and Johnny at the same time.

"Maria doesn't like it when people sit that way." She shot Johnny the die look. He shrugged. "Not my circus. I am not aware of drugs being produced around here. Why did the bureau bring me in?"

"I. Don't. Know." She could feel her jaw tighten. "Maybe Victor—"

"Victor doesn't do drugs," Alia motioned for Johnny to drop his voice, to which he ignored. "He won't touch the distribution even. Not his style."

"So, what is his style?" Alia stared Johnny in the eye. His grin morphed into a smile with teeth.

"Ah, Victor's style. Who can say," he shrugged, "Long ago legend has it he started in the bootleg business, one day he went legitimate. You are aware that he owns three or four restaurants in this area."

Of course, I know that, you ass. "Yes, I am aware of Victor's business dealings. I was curious to identify if he had other income streams."

"Not in the sector you are investigating." Johnny began to drum with one hand on the table. "I agreed to help. What do you need from me? Muscle? Arm candy?" He wiggled his eyebrows. "Introductions? What?"

"I don't think that Lucy would like the arm candy idea, and no, I do not need you to be my muscle." Alia took in a deep breath, "Alister wants the two of us to look into the Lyme connection. The two of us together will draw less suspicion—"

"Especially since the Salvi situation—"

"Exactly. We can scope it out this afternoon if you want." She slid a folder across the table. Johnny's mouth read the first few pages. Halfway down the second, his eyes rose to meet hers.

"Are you kidding me?"

"I wish I was." He ran his free hand over his face.

"I had no clue. Shit." Both sat in silence for a beat. "Yeah, I am in. Meet you at Lucy's round two?" The waitress magically appeared. She handed Johnny a check that he signed. He dropped a five on the table as he stood. "Two o'clock," he repeated.

Harlot's grace

Johnny left the same way he arrived, with hugs and handshakes. She followed as the crowd cleared.

L.M. Pampuro

Salvi Giovani paced inside the well-worn strip of oriental rug that stretched down the middle of his office. In his left hand, the weight of an ornate jewelry box. His right gestured along with the mumblings that escaped from his lips.

His office door opened to Harlot Grace, his current assistant. He hired Gracie, as he liked to address her, away from Louie's Afternoon Burlesque Show and Luncheon Buffet up in the north meadows of the city. He made the employment offer the morning after Alia turned him down. He needed a sure yes, and Gracie had always been his sure thing.

He turned his back on the six-foot buxom beauty. He could feel her breast rest on his back as she kneaded his shoulder muscles with her magical fingers. A sigh escaped his lips.

"That's okay, baby. Let it all out," she murmured in his ear. Her finger flowed from the tops of his shoulders up into the back of his neck. She stopped short of his hairline. "Tell me what you need."

A half groan escaped at the same moment his door banged against the wall. Both jumped. Gracie smoothed her skirt as she skittered passed the older version of Salvi, who took up most of the doorway.

"Salvi," he bellowed.

"Father." Salvi accepted his father's outstretched arms. "Good to see you. Is this business or--"

"Of course, this is business," he said. "Why else would I be here in the middle of the day?" The older man moved around to the executive chair behind the desk. With his back turned, he missed his son's eyes narrow.

"Salvi," he began, "I love you like my son—"

"I am your son."

"Good thing because you'd be fired if you weren't." The silence got heavy. Salvi raised an eyebrow. "You have no idea what I went through to get you this position."

"Yeah, mom said to give the boy—" His father's hand came swiftly over the desk. Harlot Grace jumped at the sound of the slap.

"Your mother runs the house. I run the company." He righted himself in the chair. "And this company has always been legitimate. Since day one!" His voice raised. "If you think I am going to let you tarnish our good name," he pointed one finger at Salvi's face, "you are wrong. Dead wrong."

The older man's eyes darkened. Salvi had seen this expression before, focused on others, not on blood. "Dad," he said. He gestured his palms up in his father's direction.

"Don't dad me. Just do what you are supposed to do. My father built this company. It supports your mother, sisters, aunts, uncles, cousins, you, and me, along with all the schmoes we employ. Do the right thing." He rose from the chair.

Salvi followed his father to the door. Outside, Harlot Grace's hands floated above the keyboard. She flashed a smile in the direction of the two men.

Giovani senior gave her a quick nod as he moved past. Salvi crooked his finger in her direction. She followed him into his office. Her high heeled shoe kicked the door closed behind.

The aerial photographs proved correct as Alia and Johnny hiked from the public parking lot by the pond back to the houses along the narrow dirt road. Cold temperatures combined with overcast skies kept both the mosquitoes and other people away. They walked at a moderate pace—Johnny's audible breath behind her.

"Let's start at the big house," Alia consulted her phone as she walked towards a yellow trail marker. "This should get us within fifty-yards."

"And then what?"

"We bushwhack the other fifty through the woods?" She raised an eyebrow at Johnny. "Why? What were you thinking?"

"Ticks, but that is beside the point." Alia grinned. "If we walk along the road, we can make out each property—"

"We can do that on the way back." Alia moved down the trail. Behind her, Johnny swore yet followed. The well-worn path curved around to the right and gave beautiful glimpses of the secluded pond. In between the lush green and yellow surroundings, birds chirped, crickets creaked, yet they appeared to be the only human disturbance.

As the terrain remained flat, Alia increased her pace. Johnny's labored breaths kept step. Twenty minutes later, she stopped in the middle of the trail. Off to her left, a meadow of shiny almond-shaped leaves formed a barrier as it wove in and out of an out of place tall iron fence.

"Damn it," Alia swore under her breath.

"Alister," Johnny panted, "would not like that language." Alia raised her middle finger in response to his comment. "Oh, I can get up through that." Alia grabbed his arm as he shifted towards the bush.

"Are you allergic to poison ivy?" He mouthed, yes. "Those leaves are growing around the fence..." she let her voice trail off.

"Huh."

"Go ahead and say it. I can see you want to," Alia threw her arms up, "we should have taken the road."

Johnny stuck his tongue out and gestured as if to bite it. He moved further along the trail. Alia followed in silence. About fifty yards in, the trail split. Yellow continued to follow the pond while another path veered off to the left.

The new branch had no markings apart from the exposed dirt, and the dark green plants parted along its side. "Huh," Johnny commented again. "We are either genuinely lucky or..."

"Or what?" Alia went in the new direction at the same moment Johnny grabbed her arm.

"Lesson number one with drug dealers—"

"You realize I have done this before—"

Johnny folded his arms across his chest. "Okay, Miss Smartypants, let's rely on your vast experience here." Alia didn't move. "We can't take this trail."

"Because it's too convenient," Alia finished his sentence. "Crap. Now What?" She rested her fingers in her hair and squeezed her eyes shut. "Let me think for a minute."

"Take your time," In between the leaves, the sky started to turn an understated shade of pink. "We probably got another hour or two of sunlight."

"We could go back the way we came."

"Could or should. Maybe we should finish our hike." Johnny pointed towards the yellow trail as it curved off to the right. "It would look better." Alia cocked her head to the side before her eyes opened wide.

"Do we have enough time before sunset?" Johnny pushed past her to continue along the yellow trail. As she passed, he swung his arm around her and planted a kiss on her cheek. "What the—"

He brought his lip around to under her ear. "Do not hit or push me away," his voice now terse. "Trust me for a minute."

L.M. Pampuro

She fell into his pace to disappear
further behind the trees.

Two baby-faced boys sat in a room that should have been someone's luxury walk-in closet surrounded by screens. On one side, the battle between good and evil played out on a 90" flat screen. The boys so close the illusion of being part of the action became more real.

On the wall to their right, the nine mounted full-color computer monitors featured images of lush green that moved with the occasional breeze. On the left, the same set up broken up between a gate, a driveway, a dirt road, several expanded lawn views, and the hallway that lead to their current position.

"Dang, man, that was a good shot," one of the kids commented into a headset microphone.

"Yeah, it was," the other responded as he held his hand up for a high five. "Oh, damn," he said as he hit pause on the game. The bottom left monitor showed two figures. They keep an eye on the two shadows as they moved back to where they started.

"Should we get—"

"No, let's wait a minute. The boss gets so cranky if we interrupt his lady time." The video game chat room exploded with comments.

Yo, you can't kill a rival and quit.

What's a matter? Mommy takes away your controller.

Man, you guys are as useless as a traffic light in GTA!

You runnin' away like a goblin in Venice!

Dang boys, you startin' to fight like Homer Simpson over a sausage sandwich.

"Hey, dude, check this out," he brought their attention back to the chatbox. When they turned back to the screen, the two figures embraced in a kiss. "Damn nature lovers." He leaned over to switch his control back on. The other boy stared at the two figures.

"That big guy looks familiar," he said at the same time he switched his control back on.

"After a while, they all do." Both brought their attention back to the most massive screen. Their fingers moved in unison, frantically over the two keyboards. The screen seeped into a dark shade of red.

Harlot's grace

Salvi pulled his trousers back up around his waist. A busty naked woman lay on the king-sized bed behind him. She stared as he dressed. "Thank you for coming out on such short notice," his voice void of emotion. "You can go back to the office now." He reached for his crisp Brooks Brothers shirt that hung on the chair. "Take the Mercedes if you want."

Harlot Grace allowed the covers to slip down to reveal her belly button. She leaned back on her warm pillow as her hand swept over the cold spot to her right, and in her heart. She caught his eye as he adjusted his Vineyard Vine light blue tie in the mirror, a gift from the F.B.I. Agent, he still wore.

She'll burn it the next time he removes it.

"Darling," her voice barely above a whisper, "can't we—"

"Not today." He cut her off mid-sentence. Her lips formed a pout as she stretched her arms over her head. The sheet moved to reveal her soft hair that steered to her lady parts. She posed again; this time, her eyes half-closed as she turned her face upward.

"I thought we could go to Mystic, have dinner, especially now that—" He turned, and she stopped short. His eyes turned dark and burned into hers.

"Take it. The. Mercedes," he punctuated each word. "Go. To. Mystic." Salvi's left eye twitched. She had pushed too far.

"No problem, honey," she said at the same time she shimmied off the bed to stand on display in front of him. He vibrated. "I'll shower and go." She grazed his arm as she walked past to grab her clothes off the dresser. When she turned to cross to the bathroom, he was gone.

Alister stood out of the news media's camera view. He listened intently as the Governor gave a statement. Three more people had turned up dead, all with the same toxicity levels as the last batch—all in Hartford proper.

"We have a few leads," he held his hand up, "yet the investigators nor I can give details since the case is on-going. I am happy to open this up to questions yet understand that I may not be able to answer." Every reporter in the room raised their hand. His press secretary indicated a small woman upfront.

"Thank you, Governor, for the briefing. Our viewers are curious as to where the investigation focuses, on the dealers themselves or higher up?"

"Thank you for that question, Ann. As of today, our focus is lateral, as our primary objective is to stop our young people from dying. Next?"

The press secretary now aimed towards an older man who leaned against the sidewall. "Yes, governor, I understand you can't give details yet under the circumstances, have the feds been brought in."

The governor gave a glance back to Alister, who returned a quick nod. "We are working with several organizations to complete the goal of getting this dangerous drug, along with the responsible parties, off the streets."

The man pushed. "So, you are saying—"

"I am saying that we are doing our best to stop our young people from dying." He gave a side glance to his press secretary.

"One more, please."

Twenty hands rose. His press secretary searched the crowd before pointing to Shane Ya, from the Hartford

Neighborhoods publications. The crowd groaned.

"Thank you, governor," he began. "There have been multiple deaths across the city. I see the local, state, and at least one federal agency present," Alister leaned further into the shadows. "Could you share your next steps, and is there anything the public can do to help?"

The governor let out a loud exhale. "Shane, if this was only this simple." He looked directly into the camera. "First to the people who have to get high, do not experiment with any new drugs at this time. Next, if you are producing narcotics in the state of Connecticut, we will find you. If you are distributing narcotics illegally in our state, we will hunt you down. No one should be told a family member overdosed because of greed. That's all."

The governor disappeared through the back door in the pressroom. Alister met him within minutes. "You do realize that you just told people who get high to stick with the tried and true."

"I did no—ah crap!" The governor moved swiftly towards his office. His state police escort in step behind. "Alister, we need to put these greedy bastards out of business, now!"

Alister shook his head yes as he veered off towards the governor's private elevator. He texted one word to both Alia and Johnny on the way to his car. *Status.*

L.M. Pampuro

The silence in the car boomed as Johnny drove up route 156 north passed the farms, firehouse, and Lyme town hall. He turned on 80 towards Hartford. Alia opened her mouth several times, shut it tight, and shook her head from side to side.

When they reach route 9, she spoke, "Are you sure you saw a camera?"

"I told you I saw a flash of red, not a camera. It could be motion sensed, but either way, someone was spying on us."

"I felt prickles on the back of my neck too."

Johnny rolled his eyes. "I didn't feel *prickles*," he stretched out the word, "I saw the infrared scope of a motion detector. I went with my training that led to a camera. How the hell did you get into the F.B.I. anyways?"

"How the hell did you get kicked out?"

"I didn't get kicked out. I resigned to go into private practice, and if I did get kicked out," he sucked in a deep breath, "Alister would have never brought me back."

Neither said a word as they moved through the lights in Middletown to merge onto I-91.

"We need to get more aerials," Alia voiced at the same time she hand wrote a list. "It is too early for a warrant, yet I would love to get a peek inside that house." Johnny pulled the car next to Alia's in the commuter parking lot. He got out at the same time.

"I think we are good," Alia put her hands up to stop him. He dropped his keys on the ground and peered under his car as he picked them up. "Klutz."

"Ah, no," he replied. "Making sure there isn't an explosive device under your car."

"Paranoid much?"

L.M. Pampuro

"Careful, and you should be too. Are you going to the office? I am going to get Lucy up to speed. She might see something we are missing."

Alia got in the car. She said a prayer as she turned over the ignition. Some days she hated this job.

Lucky Lou's office was an old closet off to the side of the stage equipped with peepholes into the dancer's lounge and monitors that focused on the bar and cash registers. His top snitch, Lester the Loser, sat alone at the far end of the bar. Loser, as Lou referred to his younger brother, had one job, to make certain the pretty boys didn't take any extra out of the till.

Thanks to the pretty boys, most days, Lester got too drunk, or lately, Lou thought, high, to give a damn what they did. Lou had a strict, yet simple, drug policy; not here. He, in truth, could give a rat's ass if someone got high, even his brother, just don't do it on his property.

He went as far as having all his employees randomly drug tested. If you didn't pass, you were gone. Lou had to fire a waitress last week for testing positive for weed. "Sorry, the rules are the rules," was his only comment. His employees did well.

Bartenders made over $100k, the waitresses a little less, and his dancers, well his dancers made more than he did.

Lou didn't mind because he made a lot of money! And it is all about the money, at least for Lou.

His attention went back to the computer screen. Someone he didn't recognize slid onto the stool next to Lester. His brother became more awake. First, the hands shifted as he shrugged. He pointed at the camera and over to the entrance. The new guy tilted his head. Lou viewed both get up to move out of the camera's focus.

He walked out into the smoke-filled room. Connecticut had banned smoking in public places years ago, yet Lou got around it by turning his home into a private club. His "members" paid a monthly fee, similar to a cover charge only a lot higher, to belong to his exclusive venue. So posh, Lou would take the fifty from anyone who can pay.

"Where'd the loser disappear to?" Lou pulled himself up on a barstool the same moment a ginger ale appeared in front of him.

"No clue. The dude walked out with one of our new members." Lou took a long sip of his drink. "And no, I know nothing about the guy. He showed up here about a week ago, paid the club fee, and never drinks. Talks to Loser."

The bartender walked to the furthest point away from Lou. He began to add ingredients into the shaker, all the while smiling and bullshitting with the person in front of him.

Lou let out a long sigh. He had bailed his brother out of many jams, hence his name. Loser had no friends, and as far as Lou knew, he had no enemies either. Lou walked down to the other end of the bar. "Send him to my office when he gets back."

Lou scrutinized the woman in a G-string and a feather boa strutting across his stage. The lunch crowd hadn't filled in, yet she attracted a dozen or so patrons. She was no Harlot, yet he gave her up to get Salvi Giovani out of his business.

The woman caught Lou's eye and gave him a quick wink, which he returned with a chin nod. "Hell of a way to make a buck," he mumbled as he moved to exit the building.

L.M. Pampuro

Alia arrived back at her apartment a little before nine at night. Johnny's mention of ticks had her take a quick shower. She put on sweats, sat cross-legged on her couch, notebook on her lap.

That fact that she missed the cameras in the trees still bothered her. Details were her thing, no matter how small. The trait fed her personality. She studied the area after Johnny's comment, yet failed to locate the red dot he insisted existed.

That bothered her too. Johnny was unyielding about the camera in the car after. He spoke to her as a child while he went on about the red light and possible tripwires. "Whoever owns that house doesn't want anyone snooping," agitated he had repeated several times. She agreed, although the why had her befuddled.

Alia proceeded to make a list. She scribbled *INCONSISTENCIES* across the top and numbered one through ten. Without a stop, she jotted down five observations. In the last spot, she wrote *Johnny DeLuca is an ass*. That line brought on a sad laugh that filled her empty room. Underneath the Johnny comment, she added, *ASK LUCY*. Lucy is Johnny's significant other. She also possessed a similar sense of curiosity as Alia.

In front of her lay, two blurred lists as her eyelids got heavy. Alia drifted off into an unsettled sleep.

Victor strolled into Lucky Lou's like he owned the place. He went straight back to Lou's closet and entered without knocking. Lou only gave a slight glance up from his computer screen as Victor took the seat across.

"To what do I owe this pleasure?" Lou asked.

"What pleasure, I came down to check-in. I note the loser is missing from the bar today."

"Yeah. He left with his new best friend."

"Male or female?" Victor's comment brought Lou's attention beyond his computer.

"Male. Not sure of much more. Can I ask about your interest in my brother?"

"Yes." Victor turned his attention to the rest of the room. On each side, hung a two-way mirror. The one on his left featured flashing lights on a stage and a half-naked woman strutting about. The one on the right appeared dark. "Why don't you have a nicer office?"

"Not everyone needs the top of a skyscraper for an office, even if it's just a Hartford skyscraper." Victor didn't laugh. "Besides, this set up affords me a view of both clubs."

"The clubs are open different hours. The location allows me to—Why am I answering you? We set this up because the pervs and the gays don't get along. One building, two clubs, two viable revenue streams. What else do we need for profit? Was there a problem with last month's financials?"

"No, no problem. All three locations can keep my wife's shopping habits going," Victor replied with a sad laugh.

"Okay, S.P., why are you here?"

"S.P., your own nickname. How cute. Yes, I am your silent partner, and my problem may not be yours," he paused for a moment, "or it might be."

"Yeah?"

Victor brought his attention back to Lou. "Why is Harlot working at my headquarters?"

"Because your son hired her."

"You understand what I mean."

"Vic, I am aware of nothing. Salvi was coming in here a couple of times a week. One day he walked into the office and said that Harlot was his new secretary. I told him great—"

"You told him great?"

"Vic, your son has an attitude problem. Thank God you never brought him into this business."

"Yes, thank God for that."

"She quit. I wished them both the best. End of story."

"Maybe. Is Harlot aware of our arrangement?"

"Harlot don't know shit. And I am certain your son didn't hire her for her typing skills if you comprehend what I mean."

Victor shifted in his chair. He leaned forward and leveled his index finger as he spoke. "Look, Louie, Salvi is an idiot, yet if he finds out I own this place and the Hump Club, it is not going be harmonious in my household. My beautiful Angelica would be devastated to find out she shopped with dirty money," he held his hand up at the same moment Lou opened his mouth. "I see what you are going to say, yet my beautiful wife has the soul of an angel. My father, God rest his soul, made me promise to keep our businesses legitimate!"

"This is a legitimate business," Lou replied. His arms now folded across his chest.

"Yes, yes, of course, yet you are aware of my domestic situation. Angelica goes to mass three times a week. She prays for us all yet..." Lou acted as if he understood Victor's logic. He's absence from a church entered multiple decades. "I can see that you understand."

"Vic, I do get it." He paused and brought his attention back to the strip club's two-way. Loser sat back in his spot. Several people walked over and slapped his brother on the back. Each waved as they walked away. He couldn't see why, yet Loser shifted in the chair after each encounter. "Hang on a minute."

Lou walked around his desk and opened the office door. He counted the number of patrons at the stage and along the bar. The bartender gave Lou a head nod in Loser's direction. He went back inside and shut the door.

"What is going on?" Victor asked. "You are pale as a Swede."

"Nothing. I am fine, Vic. So not that I don't enjoy our visits..."

"Yes, yes, I will get to the point." Lou focused more out the two-way than on Victor. "I don't like Harlot in my office."

"What do you want me to do about it? She's your son's problem now." Victor glared in his direction. "Look, Vic, Salvi hasn't come in here since she left. That is a good thing, right?" He waited for a slight acknowledgment before he continued. "Harlot is a dingbat—"

"Harlot is smarter than you think—"

"Okay, I will give you that, yet she won't be a problem."

"Okay."

"Okay?"

"If you say so," Vic follows Lou's gaze. "What about Loser?"

"What about him?"

"I told you at the start of our venture. Every place is legit. No drugs. No hookers—"

"Just good clean fun—"

"Exactly." Vic rose to leave. "And I want it kept that way or—"

"Or what," Lou stood up. His bulky frame took up space behind the desk."

"You put together our deal," Vic opened up the door, "stay on the up and up or I pull my funding. It is that simple. I want no embarrassments to my family."

The door shut. Loser sat alone, hunched over a half-empty glass. He stared into the glass and smiled. "That can't be good," Lou sighed.

L.M. Pampuro

Salvi picked up the Lladro Venus d'Milo vase by its base. On his hands and knees, a young man blocked his head with his hands. A streak of blood across the pink marble floor leads from down the hallway to where he begs.

"Salvi, I did not tell," the vase crashed down, splitting his skull. Blood pooled around his lifeless body.

A toothless grin rose across Salvi's face. Without a word, he stepped over the slumped figure. "Clean up this mess," he ordered to those within earshot. He walked down the hall to the left to create his own blood trail.

Back inside, he paced on an oriental rug, the exact copy of the one in his downtown office. His Colt 45 revolver lay in the middle of his desk. He took it in his right hand to use as a weight for a bicep curl.

"Hallway is cleaned up, boss." Salvi gave Loser a head to toe inspection. His stench of Lucky Lou's stale booze-infused the pristine office space. Loser walked over to the desk and emptied crumpled up hundreds and fifties from his pockets.

"Did you take your cut?"

"Not yet, boss. I wanted you to see the hall first. That last batch—" Salvi held up his hand, and Loser went silent. Salvi moved behind the desk, uncrumpled a few bills. His lips turned upward. "If you can give me some more, I can—"

Again, with the hand. "Anything unusual at the bar today?"

Loser thought about Vic's visit. "Nope. Nothing." Salvi divided the pile of cash in half with a slight move of his hand. Loser scooped up where he indicated and shoved the bills into the front pocket of his dirty hoodie. Adding a quick, muttered "thank you" under his breath. He waited for Salvi to give instructions. When none came, he turned and left.

Alister tapped his pen as Alia and Johnny raised their voices to each other across the top of his desk.

"Alister, if there are cameras on the property, we can assume there is something there. Can't we obtain a probable cause warrant?"

"No, you can't," Johnny interrupted. "You need cause and having a security system doesn't qualify—"

"I know what qualifies, dimwad. Now if you would let me finish—"

"There is no reason to resort to name-calling—" Alia's scream could be heard down the hall. All jumped as Alister's secretary slammed the door shut.

"Are we done?" Alister asked. He leaned forward on the desk. Both nodded yes yet still breathed hard. "Okay. Alia is aware that we can't procure a warrant she is thinking aloud. I am used to this," he turned to Johnny, "you are not."

He waited for Johnny to acknowledge this. He reached into his front drawer, pulled out a remote, and turned on a screen on the opposite wall. All shifted in their seats for a view.

"These are the photos we received before the drone was shot to pieces." On the screen appeared a large white house with a green tint. A circular stone driveway featured a black Mercedes S-class coupe, a black Denali, and an older red Mustang convertible. Off to the side, a four-bay garage with smoke wafting out the chimney.

The next photo had a more comprehensive view. An iron fence appeared and disappeared through the trees. The roof sported some type of transmitter, along with solar panels. Another rooftop with a shiny surface reflected sunlight back into the camera.

"Can you go back to the driveway?" Alia asked. She stared at the cars. "That Mercedes is familiar."

Johnny leaned forward on his elbows. "Wait for it," he said, as he reached for his cellphone. Without excusing himself, he jumped in on the conversation. "Babe, would you do your magic and see if the Giovani's have insurance on a property in Lyme." He waited a minute. "Yeah, Lyme, Connecticut."

Alia waited for Alister to explain. "This is what the drone found. Johnny," he directed the conversation, "the house isn't in Giovani's name. It belongs to," he shuffles through the folder in his hand, "the Pretty Boy Corporation, I kid you not."

"Who owns the P.B.C.?"

"I got the kid working on it." The kid Alister referred to is the latest addition to the office, sixteen, and a wiz with a computer. "He's going through the minutia now. We should have something by the end of the day."

"Is he actually that good?"

Alister expressed amusement. "We found this kid because he hacked into our computers," both gave a compulsory shutter. "I know, right? We brought him in for questioning. He showed us how he did it, and here is the best part," Alister let out a laugh, "he tells us how to set a firewall to stop hackers, like him!"

Johnny and Alia glance at each other as Alister moves his head from side to side as he laughs out loud. "What makes you think—"

"He wouldn't set us up. I brought in our expert, and he agreed with the kid. So now, we got our "intern" "new guy" whatever, who we pay a decent wage for an adult, never mind a sixteen-year-old. We promised his mom that her son's indiscretions will not appear on his permanent record so he can still attend Dartmouth in the fall."

"I have no reply to this," Alia replied.

"Yeah, babe," both turned to become aware of Johnny still on the phone. "Yep, I understand it. Thanks. Meet me at the boat? Of course, we can go to Bill's. Chow, Bella." Johnny hit the end call. "Oh, she said that Giovani's did not insure the house but based on the plate information I gave her, all three of those cars—"

"Are owned by Salvi Construction."

"I knew I recognized that Mercedes." Both men did an eye-roll behind her back. "What's the plan?" Alia stood and stretched. "Because Salvi's companies are all legitimate. And," she paused for effect, "drugs wouldn't be their thing. The father needs to be a pillar in the community. That goes back to the grandfather and the way they were treated when they first arrived in this country."

"True. But Salvi is different from his father and grandfather," Johnny indicated. "Should we pay him a visit?"

"Unfortunately, we need cause first," Alister reminded. "Right now, all we have is dead bodies."

"Are there more?"

"Two in the hospital died this morning, and there was another surge in Hartford last night. The Governor is off the wall, and I can't blame him. The protesters are off the wall, and I can't blame them." Alister turned his full attention to Alia and Johnny, "Let's finish this. Alia—"

"Do I have to?"

"Put on those big girl panties, sista," Johnny expressed amusement. Alia pulled out her phone and hit send.

"Salvi Giovani, please."

Harlot's grace

L.M. Pampuro

Harlot didn't like it that Salvi's perfect ex waited in front of her to see her current man. She hated it even more than the woman kept trying to start a conversation. Harlot stared at her computer screen to pull her full concentration to the solitaire game only she could see. She moved her mouse and typed a few keystrokes.

To Alia, Salvi's secretary seemed engrossed in her work, or she would have if the computer game she played didn't reflect off the framed photo on the wall behind her. Every few minutes, Alia would ask a question. The response came back short, curt, yet polite. She opened her mouth to try again at the same moment, Salvi's door opened.

He stood in the frame dressed to the nines in her favorite Brooks Brothers navy gray suit. With it, he wore the Vineyard

Vines tie she gave him a few months ago. It matched perfectly! His eyes warmed as they met hers. Wordlessly he swept his hands across the threshold to invite her into his space.

She stood to make a production of pulling the hem of her skirt down. Although the length remained the same, both Salvi and Harlot's gaze drew up and down her legs. With a slight wiggle, she strutted by Salvi, who closed the door after, without a backward glance.

Alia took a seat on the couch in the corner. She waited for Salvi to join her. "To what do I owe this pleasure?" he asked as his eyes undressed her.

"I wouldn't use the word pleasure," Alia said. "I think I hit your car."

"You think?"

"Well, it looked like your car. You know, there aren't that many S Coupes on the road up here, but let me tell you the strange part," Salvi waited as Alia adjusted herself, "I have a new friend who likes to hike," she waited for a reaction. "We were hiking in a state park last weekend, and as we were leaving, my friend thought it would be fun to spin his tires…"

"Spinning tires is funny? How old is your new friend, Alia?"

"No matter," she replied with a wave. "So, we were leaving some Indian name state forest, and a car like yours comes up fast on the dirt road as my friend is spitting up rocks. I know for a fact that the rocks hit the car because the driver swerved and well…"

"Well, what?"

"Well, we took off. So, I thought I would come to confess that I wrecked your car." Salvi studied Alia. He waited for a beat to let out a loud, hearty laugh.

"Alia, if you wanted to see me, you could have come up with a better excuse! Come here, baby." He reached across the couch as she slipped out of reach.

"Salvi, I am serious. This happened. I didn't want you to think—"

"Didn't want me to think what? Alia, you show up at my office with an unbelievable story, and you think I am making up shit? Oh baby," he runs his hands through his slick black hair. "Why are you here?" His eyes go dark, and his tone changed from playful to direct.

Alia moved towards the door. "I thought I. I mean I seriously. Salvi, you are right. I shouldn't have come here. I mean seriously, why would your car be on a dirt road in Nehantic State Forest," his expression changed. "I must be seeing things."

"Yes, you must. Next, you'll be telling me you saw a red Mustang there too." Alia doubled up as the acid in her stomach turned.

"Yeah, right," she placed her hand on the door handle. "And a purple Beamer too." She opened the door a crack. "Salvi, I am sorry to have bothered you. I must be going crazy."

His face showed no emotion, and his eyes had gone dead. "Stay out of the woods, Alia," he said. "They can be deadly places."

Alia stopped in her tracks as Salvi's lip turned up. His smile never reached any further. She gave him an awkward hug and left. Salvi waited until silence filled the lobby area. "Get me the loser," he barked at Harlot.

Alia ran from the corner over to Johnny's car. She threw open the door and dove into the passenger's seat. "Go," she said. Johnny waited until the building disappeared behind another to speak.

"How did it go?" He noticed Alia had her arms crossed as she held her waist.

"Fine," she answered. "Really freaking fine. Johnny, we are in deep crap." His right eyebrow raised. His eyes not leaving the road. "Salvi denied being in the woods, of course, BUT, and mean big BUT, he flippantly said that next, we'd be seeing a red Mustang."

"A red Mustang, huh?" Johnny blew out a long breath. "I need to talk with Victor."

"Victor, not Salvi?"

He pushed a few buttons on his cellphone. "Lucy, it's me—"

"And Alia," Alia jumped in.

"Hi, Al came over the speaker. What do you guys need?"

"Quick question, the red Mustang, was that part of the Matteo Corporation fleet?"

"The one from the photo? Yeah. I forget who is primary. I think it is one of the secretary's, though I can't tell you who's since Victor gives all the secretaries of the company officers use of the cars, or at least he has in the past."

"That's all I needed. Thanks, babe." Johnny disconnected. His fist hit the steering wheel. "Shit. I had hoped I was wrong. We need to talk to Alister and Victor."

"I call dibs on Alister," Alia said.

"Together. We need to talk together."

L.M. Pampuro

Lou turned up the volume on the microphone he had installed under the lip of the bar in front of Loser's usual perch. The loud music from the stage drowned out many of the voices, yet through his new five-hundred-dollar earphones, he could make out parts of conversations.

The installer insisted that hooking into a transcript program would be futile because of the noise level, yet Lou had him do this anyway. *Pour Some Sugar On Me* lyrics repeated every hour across the screen. "Freakin' hate Def Leopard," Lou muttered as he deleted another round from the transcript. He also got rid of drink orders and small talk.

Through the mirror, he kept under surveillance Harlot, as she strutted into the bar. Many patrons turned away from the stage to acknowledge the diva with whistles and applause. She smiled and lifted her blouse to flash one ample breast in their direction. Harlot strutted to the end of the bar to park her tiny rear end on the seat between Loser and the wall.

Lou turned up the microphone.

"Hi, Sweetie," Harlot's squeaky voice came through. "Buy a lady a drink?"

"I would if I saw one," Loser answered. The sound of flesh hitting flesh came through Lou's earphones. On the monitor, Loser rubbed his cheek.

"I will only ask—"

"Give the Lady a drink on my tab," Loser tapped the bar in from of Harlot. "Why are you here?" Lou focused on the monitor as he waited on her answer. His bartender brought her a glass of cheap champagne and tried to jump into a conversation with Harlot. Loser cut him off. "Yeah, thanks for the drink, Buddy. Don't you have work to do?"

The bartender held up his middle finger as he walked to the opposite end. "That was unnecessary," Harlot stated.

"You didn't answer my question."

Harlot's eyes darted around the room. She stared straight into one of the cameras. "Where is Lou?"

"Probably in his office jerking off. Why are you here?"

"Can he see us?"

"No." Lou snickered. His brother had no clue.

"Salvi is freaking out. He's been smashing anything he can get his hands on. I'm scared." She leaned in to rub her breasts against Loser's side.

"Salvi isn't my problem," he replied as his eyes started to glaze over. A bit of drool escaped from his mouth as Harlot reached her hand below the bar to rest on his upper thigh.

"I am, in fact, scared. That girl, his ex, came to visit and said she hit his Mercedes or one that looked like his, when she was hiking," she paused for a moment, "in Lyme." Loser reached down to stop her hand from moving over his jeans.

"Say what?"

"You heard me. Salvi is on a tear. He destroyed his office. Vases! Pictures! Anything not attached. I left after he ordered me to clean up his mess. I called a cleaning crew and got the hell out of there.

He's been blowing up my phone, and if you'd look," Loser already had his phone out, "he's probably blowing up yours too."

On the screen, he had ten missed calls, all from the same number. Harlot jumped back. "Shit," escaped her lips at the same moment, the door to the club flung open.

Salvi's shadow stretched across the room to where they sat. In two strides, he positioned himself in their space. He had a baseball bat in one hand. The other clinched into a fist. Def Leopard screamed through the speakers, yet silence reverbed throughout the club.

Lou turned up the volume with his left hand while he punched Victor's digits in his phone with his right. The bartender took two strides over to the register. His hand reached below at the same time something metal met his temple.

"Push it, and I will splatter your brains across that wall," another figure, dressed head to toe in black, outstretched a hand that held a small handgun. "Let's sit over here," he moved towards the two stools at the end of the bar, "and watch." Near the door stood two others at attention in the same uniform. Their hands crossed in front of their crotches. Both are holding the same handgun.

"Fancy freakin' meeting you here," Salvi reached across the bar as Harlot dunked into the shadow. Salvi screeched as his free hand hit the wall where her head leaned moments earlier. "Merda!" he screamed at the same time he swung the bat along the bar top. Glasses shattered. Liquid sprayed across anything within reach.

Loser stood to block his path.

"Salvi," Loser's voice came out calm and level. He grunted as Salvi's fist jammed into his stomach.

"Loser," Salvi spat back. He pushed him aside with the tip of the bat to perch himself on the bar stool in the middle. "Jack Daniels straight up and whatever these two are drinking," he called to the bartender, who rose slowly. The other followed close behind. "Is Lou here?" Both shrugged. "Doesn't matter. Did either of you talk to Alia?" Both moved their heads from side to side. The bartender placed a glass of amber liquid in front of Salvi. He downed it in a single shot. "We need to kill her."

"Kill who?" Loser caught Harlot shaking her head no behind Salvi.

"Alia."

"Your ex? Breaking up isn't exactly…" The slap came swiftly. Loser fell to the floor. He wiped the blood dripping from his nose across his hand up to his elbow.

"Not because she dumped me, you idiot because she was in Lyme. She knows. I know she knows." Salvi jumped up. He swung the bat in circles as he continued to mumble, "she knows."

"She is FBI," Loser said.

"What the hell did you say?" Salvi had the butt of the bat under Loser's chin. He pushed up hard.

"Alia works for the FBI," Loser mumbled. Salvi swung the bat down hard on Loser's shoulder. He repositioned himself to extend across the bar to take out a row of glassware. Behind him, patrons scattered.

"Who else knows?" he sputtered.

"Knows about what?" Lou's voice cut in as all three jumped. Salvi took in a deep breath as he turned to stare Lou down.

"None of your damn business," he said as he grabbed Harlot by the wrist. "You're with me," he stated as he pulled her off the barstool, towards the door. "Loser, step on it."

"What was—"

"I got to go—" Lou grabbed his brother by the arm.

"Where?"

"Doesn't matter," Loser turned to embrace Lou. He squeezed his eyes shut with the same intensity he hugged his brother. Loser broke the hold to limp out the door.

Johnny Deluca enjoyed his espresso as he read the latest report on the Lyme property. He was against Alia confronting Salvi, yet no one had listened. There were three more deaths, along with ten more people admitted to the psychiatric ward. All had similar toxins in their system.

The Lyme property held the answers, at least in his mind. Salvi Giovani's car had been seen there twice in drone photos. He had Lucy, his partner, looking for the offshore accounts. To date, his wealth wasn't out of character, as far as anyone could see.

He gathered up all the papers to stuff into an old file folder and dropped a five on the table. On the way out, he hugged each lady who stood by the door. He smiled at the chatter about what a nice boy he is like the sunlight from the open door temporarily blinded him.

Out on the street, Johnny's eyes adjusted to catch Victor Giovani, leaving Gino's place across the street. Johnny knew the two were associates, yet one's business played out in the shadows while the other's appeared more legal. Victor caught Johnny's stare.

He waited a minute before he walked across the avenue to where Johnny stood. "Enjoying an espresso?" Victor asked.

"Beautiful day to be out and about," Johnny replied. He waited as Victor reached in his coat pocket for a thin cigar. He offered one to Johnny, who declined.

"Words is you are working for the feds again," he said as he lit up. Johnny replied with a head shake. "Gino says—"

"Gino told you I was working for the feds?" Johnny interrupted.

"Gino said we need to do something to keep these kids from killing themselves," he finished. When Johnny didn't comment, Victor added, "Do you have a clue?"

"A couple." A beep came from Victor's pocket. He ignored the noise.

Johnny opened his mouth to speak as there was another. The notifications kept coming. "Shouldn't you check that?"

Victor blew out another long spiral of smoke. He rested the cigar on the side of a flowerpot to reach into his pocket. "*Merde*," he sighed. "Excuse me," he held up one finger as he spoke into the phone. "What do I owe the pleasure?"

Johnny moved to walk away at the same moment. Victor began to swear in Italian. "*Culo stupido! Cazzo idioto!*" Victor grabbed Johnny's arm, then held up one finger. "I will be right there." He threw his phone against the sidewalk to send plastic and glass shards in every direction.

Johnny stood perfectly still.

"*Mio figlio e un idioto!*"

"Which one?" Johnny asked. Victor let out a tirade of swears. Old ladies made u-turns on the sidewalk. The ladies walked backward into the café they had exited. Across the street, Gino's henchmen stood, arms folded, outside of the Italian club.

"Which one do you think?" Victor waved at Gino's guards. He grabbed Johnny's upper arm. "Come on with me."

Johnny disconnected himself. "No. Not until you tell me—"

"My idiot son beat the crap out of Lou's brother. The two took off together. Lou said that the idiot also trashed our bar." Johnny raised an eyebrow. "Like you weren't aware," Victor barked. "We need to go to the club."

"I'll follow you," Johnny said as he stopped in front of his BMW SUV.

"Fine." Victor directed to his Cadillac Escalade. "Have your partner meet us there. And Alister too."

"Lucy?"

"No, Alia. My dumb ass son is going to kill her." Victor stopped traffic with an illegal u-turn. Johnny did the same right behind him.

"Call P.I.T.A.," he instructed as he drove. The number rang before it skipped straight to voice mail. "Alia, Johnny. Find Alister and head to Lucky Lou's as soon as you get this. We have a situation."

The tires screeched as he pulled onto I-91 towards the north meadows.

Harlot's grace

Alia opened her shower curtain to Salvi and another man leaning inside her bathroom door. Her phone rang in the distance.

"What the hell!" she screamed as she pulled the fabric back to surround her naked body. Salvi's lips crept up into a smile. She opened her mouth to scream.

"Don't bother with the theatrics," Salvi said. He ran his eyes up and down her naked body. She pulled back into the shower stall to add distance. "There is no one here to hear you besides my associate and me." He gestured towards Loser.

"Why are you here? And how did you get into my apartment?" Her heartbeat increased. She tried to slow breath as her trainer had taught. Her head spun. "I repeat—"

"How did you find out about my house in Lyme?" Salvi used a soothing voice that caught Alia off guard.

"You have a house in Lyme?" He raised his hand to lower it as quickly. His eyes bore into hers.

"Alia, my love," Loser snorted behind him, "I need you to tell me how you found out about the Lyme house?"

Loser stuck his finger into her moisturizer, smelled it, and spread the remains on her sunshine guest towel. He began to do the same with her face cream.

"Can you tell your friend to stop sticking his hands into my stuff?" Salvi turned to chin point towards the door. Loser disappeared from view. He brought his attention back to Alia. He reached for the curtain. "No!"

"Tell me," he said as he grabbed on to her arm. "Tell me now!" Her phone rang again in the distance. Salvi smiled. "That would be the man you took into the forest?" He tugged her closer. "Your friend who hikes?"

Alia brought her arm up to shrug out of his grip. He let loose his hold. She brought her to stand up to full height as she stepped over the top of the tub. Water dripped off her body to form a puddle on the tiled floor. Salvi leaned his body in close. He raised his hand to brush a drip off her cheek yet said nothing. His eyes locked tight on hers.

"My love, there is fear on your face, which shows you are a smart woman." A pair of jeans and a t-shirt dropped inside the door. "So smart that you will put those clothes on and come with my associate and me. We will go for a ride—"

"And if I refuse?"

"I will haul your naked ass out to my car and have my associate ride in the back seat with you," he paused, "at least for a little while." She reached around him to pick up her old Allman Brothers t-shirt from her 26th birthday show. She slid the shirt over her head. Although covered, the shirt left no mystery to her breast size.

Of course, there was no bra or underwear. "I can't wear those jeans. Let me get a pair of sweats." Alia tried to push passed Salvi.

"Would this be in your sweat drawer?" Loser held out her Glock 23. Salvi pushed passed her.

"What do we have here, my love?"

"Glock 23 semi-automatic," Loser answered. "Standard issue." No one said a word.

"Put on the jeans, Alia," Salvi said as he turned the gun over in his hand.

"This is not how it looks. I am a single woman living alone. I needed protection in this neighborhood. My grandfather gave that to me before he died."

"Did grandpa work for the feds?" Alia shook her head no.

"That is a new model, boss," Loser added.

"When did grandpa die, Alia?" Without a word, she pulled the jeans over her behind as she attempted to adjust the crotch around her lady parts. "We have another mystery, my friend. Loser, let's take my former fiancé out to our country house," his voice hysterical. "And have fun as we drive there."

Salvi led Alia out her front door, into a black SUV that waited at the bottom of her steps. Loser got in the back seat with her while Salvi walked around to the front passenger side.

He glanced back at her apartment door. "Loser, did you grab her phone?" The driver hopped out, ran up the stairs. He returned moments later. Four missed calls, yet no numbers appeared on the screen.

He threw the phone out the window. "No sense in being tracked," he gestured to the driver. Her phone smashed against the pavement at the same moment; Loser leaned over her.

Victor and Johnny arrived in a parking lot that contained Lou's 1968 Camaro along with an older BMW. They walked into the bar side by side. No music played. The house lights illuminated the damage.

Piles of broken glass leaned up against the bar as the stools scattered between the back row of tables. The place smelled like old whiskey, sour beer, and something that couldn't be identified yet pervaded through the lingering booze. Johnny put his hand over his nose.

"He took the loser," Lou's strained voice cut through the silence. Victor and Johnny focused on the outline of a figure who sat at a booth in the shadows of the empty stage. "Said something about killing a broad, too."

A whiff of marijuana passed by. Johnny got a chill. "What broad?" he asked. Lou shrugged, yet they both missed the gesture. "Who?" Johnny repeated.

"His ex, I think. I was more worried about the fit that was damaging our bar along with him dragging off my brother." Victor let out a deep sigh. "I forgot you were here," Lou's face lit up in the flame of his lighter. He took a deep drag off his Unbreakabowl before he continued, "This is Salvi, Victor. Harlot went too. The three of them, together."

Lou slid out of the booth. He straightened chairs as he walked around the tables. Each chair moved along the old wood floor sent a chill through the room. He joined the others near the bar. Both turned towards Johnny.

"What are you looking at me for?" His right thumb moved across the keyboard of his phone as his left hand rested on his hip. "Any damage to the other club?" he asked without looking up.

"No," Lou answered. "Salvi came in, bat in hand. He brought three others. One held a gun to my bartender's head while the other two stood at the door. All carried. Salvi proceeded to clear the few glasses on the bar. That is when I went to my office door. He walked over to the Loser and Harlot. Smacked him, tried to strangle her. Yelled something about killing his ex. Smashed more of my liquor bottles. And left." Lou's breathing now ragged.

"Call Allister," Victor instructed Johnny.

"You are bringing in the Feds on your own son?" Lou shook his head. "Are you kidding me?"

"Lou, the boy is out of control. I can't have him acting like a *teppista*."

"Yeah, but Victor, can't we go to Gino or someone in the south end?"

"Gino wouldn't touch this mess," Johnny said. "Alister is on his way. They're going to want to view the tape."

"What tape?"

"Come on, Lou, you've got this place better wired than a grocery store. Next door too." Johnny paused for a reaction. Stillness met him. "Lou, they only care about Salvi at this point. If there is anything else going on here—"

"We run a legitimate business," Victor interjected. "I don't like what you are insinuating."

"I am not insinuating anything." Johnny glanced at his keyboard. "I got to go find Alia," he added as an afterthought, "and the others. Victor, I will be in touch."

"Where are you going?" Victor asked. "This is my son we are talking about. I should go with you."

"No, you stay here with Lou. Talk to Alister."

"Where are you going?" Lou asked.

"Lyme."

L.M. Pampuro

Loser carried Alia's limp body up the marble staircase. "Put her in the guest bedroom," Salvi instructed. She had passed out at the same moment his hand slip under her blouse. Her lack of fight took away his desire, yet later, as Salvi said, they would try the new batch on her.

The drugs seemed to perk up the testers, at least for a little while. Loser dropped Alia on top of the black quilt. He left the room. In the stillness, Alia began to move. Her eyes darted around. Once a sense of place kicked in, she relocated her body to a sitting position. The bed squeaked quietly with each motion.

Floor to ceiling windows provided a view of a lush green forest. Shadows indicated she lay on the East side of the property. In the distance, she could hear voices yet couldn't make out the words.

She pushed herself off the bed to try the door. Locked. The handle hot in her hand. She next tried the windows. Both bolted shut. Two other doors led to dead ends. One a closet with a brown crusty substance on the rug in the middle. The other a luxurious marble bathroom with a sunken tub. Something foul floated near the drain.

"Obviously, the maid is on vacation," Alia mumbled.

She walked back in the first room and stood in the window. The location overlooked the poison ivy-covered iron fence she and Johnny had stood near. At least it appeared that way to her. A red flash caught her eye in the trees. "A camera, I'll be damned. Johnny was right." Instead of positioned towards the woods, the camera now aimed its focus at her window.

Alia raised her middle finger in its direction.

Downstairs, Salvi took over the monitor room. He repositioned all the cameras on Alia, except one. The final screen flashed on and off the road to the house. Any movement, including birds and small animals, turned the camera on.

He spied on his ex-lover surveyed her surroundings. He noted her disgust as she came in contact with the dried blood and other fluids from his last guest. "Oh, the weight of being a businessman," he sighed.

"What, boss?" Loser stuck his head in the door.

"Nothing. Not a thing." Salvi shifted in his chair. "Our guest is awake."

"Is it time to play?"

"Keep it in your pants, Loser. At least for now. How is the latest batch coming?"

"Should be ready in about an hour."

"An hour, you say? Do you want to play now or wait?"

"Hey boss," he grabbed his crotch, "I always want to play. They are more fun right after the dose..." Loser's eyes glazed over.

"Where is Harlot?"

"She's in your room. I put the trigger switch on in case she wanders, yet left the doors open."

"Good, good. No phones, right?"

"No phone, boss." Salvi turned back to the screen. Alia sat on the edge of the bed, hands folded in front. Her eyes half shut; her mouth moved as if in conversation. "Should have wired that room too."

"You did, boss." Loser stepped around to flip a button. "We wired every room except yours." His attention went to Alia. "I think she is praying."

"Alia? No, Alia doesn't pray. She doesn't even go to church on Sunday." The two stared at the screen for a few more minutes. "Speaking of redemption, it is time for Harlot to redeem herself with me. Maybe we can put a speaker on in the guest room after we start going at it so Alia can enjoy the sounds of Gracie and me?"

"Consider it done, boss." Loser disappeared to return a few minutes later with a small portable speaker. "Hit this switch, and I will put it through."

L.M. Pampuro

Salvi walked up the stairs, the speaker in one hand, the other tucked into his waistband.

Johnny Deluca sped through the curves on route 156 as he listened to Lucy's description of the property from the small camera he had left in the wooded area he and Alia hiked.

"I can see your girlfriend in the second window on the top floor."

"She's not my girlfriend, you are. What else? Is there anyone with her?"

"Whatever. Not as far as I can see. She gave the Italian salute to the woods—"

"Not the woods. She must have finally noticed the camera in the trees."

"Yep, she's a bright one."

"Lucy, stop. What else do I need to know?"

"Besides Salvi and the Loser, there is another woman there. Also, I think something is going on in the garage area.

There is bright white smoke billowing up from that direction."

"Billowing?" Johnny laughs.

"Hey, I have the boring part here. What's next?"

"Call Alister and give him the update. Tell him we located Alia and, most likely, the lab."

"Anything else?"

"Yeah, send in the troops." Johnny let out a long sigh.

"Hey babe, be careful."

"Always, my love. Always."

Salvi walked into his bedroom. Harlot sat back on the bed, book in hand. She glanced up with his arrival.

"Hi," she said as she sat there wide-eyed.

"What are you reading," Salvi sat beside her on the bed. He switched the speaker on as he moved it to the nightstand behind him.

"Nothing," she said as she placed the book behind her. "Just a dilatory effort while waiting for you."

"Dilatory?"

"Yeah, it means to procrastinate. I am trying to up my vocab."

"Well, babe, let's dilatory no more." He rolled his body on top of hers.

L.M. Pampuro

From down the hall, the grunting and panting echoed in Alia's room. The high volume had her lying on her side with pillows placed on both ears. As she positioned herself to reduce the sound, it became louder to shake the walls.

"He's not that good," she muttered as she pressed harder on her ears to drown out Harlot's wails. Alia ran into the bathroom and shut the door, for a little relief. Her head pounded to the rhythm of background noise.

She slid down on the floor at the same moment the room went silent. With a loud sigh of relief, Alia rose to re-enter the bedroom. The grunts and wails slipped through the walls at an ear-piercing volume. She ran back into the bathroom and slammed the door.

Salvi left Harlot in the center of the bed; her clothes half ripped; tears chased each other through her makeup to create streams of sadness. A ragged breath not from satisfaction, but confusion. His fingers left red marks pressed into her neck. Her clothes torn up from a wild animal.

Harlot's grace

Yet Harlot knew an act when she saw one. Down the hall, her wails still echoed, though her mouth lay silent, except for an occasional hard intake of air.

Johnny drove down the dirt road and parked in the same spot he and Alia shared earlier. His eyes scanned the trees and bushes for red dots or other indications that someone kept the area under observation.

In Johnny's world, someone always watched.

Within minutes the parking area filled with black Ford S.U.V.'s along with a couple of Jeeps. He leaned against his vehicle as two drones launched in the direction of the house. Overhead a helicopter hummed. Alister spoke and coordinated action as each group arrived. Across the lot, he gave Johnny a quick head nod as he moved in his direction.

"Drone is getting footage now," Alister said. The two jumped at a gunshot followed by an explosion. Alister ran his hand over his face, "Correction, the drone is inoperable."

"Probably not the best idea to fly that thing," Johnny noted. Neither said a word. A team member ran over and held a small screen.

"Same cars in the driveway, boss," Alister cringed at the title, "and Alia is in the same place."

"Where did the gunshot come from?" The kid gave Johnny the stare down. "I asked you a question?" he repeated.

"Working on it."

"You don't have an angle?" Johnny turned away.

"Thank you," Alister said. "Please inform me immediately if you find any other information." The kid stood there for another beat. "You still here?" He turned and left.

"Alister,"

"We have work to do in his office attitude."

"You think?"

"Please, I know. He is new to the team." The kid strolled back over to a small group, all on screens. He stood off to the side. "He's supposed to be a computer genius." Johnny's laugh cut through the other noise. "You, however, should be aware."

"Doesn't matter," he said as he waved his hand towards the group. "I'm going up the road in by the front entrance. There's smoke coming from that side, the garage?" Johnny got a nod from Alister. "Team one will follow me. They will block off the garage and investigate. Team two is all yours. If you follow that path," he points to the trail he and Alia hiked, "it leads to the back. There are cameras set up, probably motion censored—"

"We have a third team coming in from the other side too. I got the kid—"

"Kid stays here."

"Johnny, the kid has some sort of heat tech that shows the figures inside—"

"Alister." Alister took in a deep breath and shrugged in Johnny's direction. "Please. And I would keep an eye on what exactly he has on that screen."

Both men turned to gaze at the last team member, disappear down the path. Johnny shook Alister's hand before he jumped into the back of a black pick-up truck.

The man seated next to him smiled. "Shits about to get real," the kid put a tight grip on the AK-47 across his lap.

Alia didn't move when the door hit the wall. She sat still and continued to mumble; her focus did not leave her hands, although she sensed Salvi's every shift.

He relocated in front of her, so close his foul breath coiled into her nostrils. He folded his hands to rest on his lower front, legs spread in a V shape. "I never heard you pray before," he said. His soft voice interrupted her chant. "I guess it is true that people turn to God when they are desperate."

She brought her eyes up to meet his. His blank stare greeted back. Alia mumbled something else then pushed her body up to match his stance.

Neither moved.

"You lied to me," Salvi said, "I loved you, and you lied to me."

Harlot's grace

"You cheated on me," Alia responded. "I loved you, and you cheated on me." Salvi shifted at the same moment his hand rose to touch her cheek. Alia brought hers up to hold his.

They stood in silence.

Alia gripped his hand hard as she twisted his wrist backward. Salvi's let out a high-pitched scream that rattled the house. She turned to run her left foot down his calf. Automatically, his hands went to block his groin. Her leg cocked back in a sidekick. She went high into his stomach.

Salvi fell back against the dresser. Alia jumped at the same moment his hand clung tight to her ankle.

Her face burned as it hit the rug. Salvi turned her over and raised his fist in the air. "La puttana!" he yelled as his knuckles hit her cheek. She folded back at the same time his fist raised again.

"Boss," Loser's voice froze both. They lay wide-eyed on the floor.

"What!" Salvi screamed.

"It's ready."

A deep laugh erupted from Salvi's gut. He stared down at Alia. Spit flew as he spoke. "You lied to me, la cagna. You played me for a stolto. Never again." His fist raised and fell by his side. "You are in for a treat," Salvi's voice now calm again. "Oh, what a treat! Loser," he barked, "would you grab me a tester, please."

The addition of the word please sent chills up Alia's back.

"My lady friend," Salvi let out another gut laugh, "will be part of our, oh what do doctors call this, oh yeah. You will be part of our study on this batch." He drilled his eyes into Alia's, "Our federal agency of investigation lay friend." He waited for a response.

"When did you find out?" Alia said. She struggled to breathe under Salvi's weight.

"I knew all along," he said with a wave of the hand. "I was leading you on to find out what you were up to." He cackled.

"So, you never actually loved me?"

"No." His words hurt more than they should.

Loser arrived back with a small, silver plate. On top of a little white towel lay a single syringe, half-full of a gray, murky liquid. He placed the plate on the bed. From his front pocket, Loser removed a rubber tourniquet. He put it next to the needle.

"Boss, do you want me to—"

"Yes," Salvi answered. He shifted his weight to hold still Alia's right arm. Loser tied the tourniquet and waited a minute. Like a pro, he held up the needle and tapped it twice. Alia began to move her body in any direction she could, yet her arm sat sequestered in place.

"If you move, this will hurt more," Loser wined. Salvi grabbed the needle out of the Loser's hand. With force, he thrust it into Alia's arm.

She let out a scream.

"No worries," Salvi said. "In a minute, you should feel fantastic, at least that is what they tell me." He and Loser doubled up together. "Then again, this batch is new. Maybe you fall over dead. I don't care." He shrugged as he released her body.

Both men stood to leave. "We will be back in a few. If you are still alive, well, then we'll see." The door shut. The room began to ripple in an ebb and flow pattern.

She brought her mouth onto the insertion area. She sucked as hard as she could, then spit onto the bed. Alia repeated the process two times. Her stomach began to churn as the room spiraled. "Vertigo," she muttered as she moved towards the bathroom, each lurch labored.

Her right arm clasped as her face dragged on the rug. "Water," she whispered. "Water." Her left hand came in contact with something cold. She pushed her legs to slide onto a tiled floor.

She tried to reposition herself vertically, her head much too heavy for the body that shivered and shook against the side of a clawed bath. She sunk back against the porcelain.

Alia gave a forceful lunge in the direction of the toilet. She frantically scooped the cold water over her head and into her mouth. The world around her stabilized, at least for the moment.

She kept going until her shirt clung around her breasts. She rose to balance herself on the now slippery tile. Her breath is hard.

Harlot's grace

Alia leaned her body against the heavy door. It slammed shut. One hand stabilized her head while the other turned the old fashion lock to slip inside the wall.

Voices grew on the other side, followed by banging on the door. The room began to spiral, traces of green leaves, bare-breasted women, and white sparkles flashed around her.

On the other side of the door, Salvi's voice raised above the noise and pounding on the door she leaned her body against.

L.M. Pampuro

Loser walked back to the garage, as hot as he got for women who fought back, he didn't like to view the injection process. If Alia reacted like the others, he would go prepare another dose, wait ten minutes or so, then go back for round two.

His walk turned to a skip.

Inside the garage, Loser studied the two chemists in border shorts crusted with rust color substance remove a smoking liquid from a makeshift still. Both wore ski goggles and protective gloves, along with old kitchen aprons covered their chest

Loser couldn't pronounce their names. He referred to one as Kiss The Cook or KTC at times, while the other was GYB, short for Grab Your Balls. The two appeared nothing like each other, yet when they switched aprons, out of respect, Loser switched their names.

GYB waved through the glass for Loser to come in. He hated this part because his gut told him to stay out of the lab, yet the polite boy his mother raised moved him to the men's side.

"How was the last batch?" KTC bounced as he asked.

"Did the person get exceedingly high?" GYB jumped in.

"Or did they die?" Now KTC's eyes were saucers. Loser wondered how much they sampled and not for the first time, how both were still alive.

"She was droopy after," Loser said.

"Droopy? What the fuck is droopy?" GYB's head now tilted to one side. He waved his arms in the air and speak in monkey chatter, or at least that is what Salvi referred to their native tongue. The other responded back. His voice carried more of an edge. GYB twirled the smoking beaker with one hand while the other stroked his chin. "We definitely did not go for droopy."

"Maybe we need more eye of newt?" KTC giggled as he added a blue shaded fluid. The solution bubbled. "Oh, crap." GYB placed the beaker on a wood workbench at the same time KTC moved Loser to behind a glass screen.

They scrutinized in silence. When nothing occurred after a few minutes, both went back to the beaker, picked it up, and continued as if the bubbling never took place.

"So, what brings you here. Need another dose?" KTC brought his attention back to the Loser. "I can have one ready in five."

"No dose," Loser said. He opened a drawer in the red, mechanic's tool chest and selected one of the dozen mason jars inside. "I need a little smoke."

"That stuff will kill you," GYB noted.

"Yeah, and that won't," Loser said as he crumbled up a bluish-green bud of cultured marijuana into one of the organic rolling papers he kept on the side. He rolled the mixture tight then sealed the paper with a line of his saliva. "Perfection," he noted as he held the joint up for inspection.

"Can't smoke in here," GYB said. Loser slipped a tube of yellow liquid from the top of the workbench, into his pocket.

"We are about to add a highly flammable liquid," KTC added.

"You might want to leave," both said in unison. The monkey chatter got louder and more animated.

Loser's other hand already turned the knob. He waved back and lit the joint upon exit. His lungs filled with each inhale as he considered Alia laid out in the guest room. Her lying in wait did nothing for his libido. "Maybe she isn't the one," he hooted.

Behind the tall iron gate, movement caught his focus. He stared into the trees. Bark and leaves swayed—a small roach of a joint burned between his fingers. "Must be the weed," he concluded.

Johnny brought his hand up at the same moment his team froze. In the driveway of the made to appear old federal, the Loser stood smoking a joint. He moved the team back into the trees with one wave.

Loser started in their direction. "It's the weed, you idiot," Johnny whispered.

He caught a muffled snort behind him yet did not turn to address the culprit. He waited until Loser disappeared into the house to speak.

"Haz-mat guys take the garage. Do not, I repeat, do not destroy this lab. We need it intact to analyze. Based on intel, there are max four people in there. The rest follow me into the house. Priority A is finding Agent Price and getting her out. Signal to the medics if she appears drugged in any way."

"What about Salvi Giovani?" One of the no-names asked.

"Find him and arrest him, by any means possible. Do not kill him. The others in there are expendable, but not him." Johnny gave a quick nod before he brought his gaze to the sky. "This will be the last, I promise," he muttered. "Let's go," he said a bit louder.

Alister stood on the side of a dirt lot. Over to his left two hospitals on wheels, four fully loaded hummers, along with the state police crime lab, waited on instructions. Victor Giovani leaned against Alister's Crown Vic. He sipped from a cup of Starbucks, a stop he insisted be made on route.

Several men in camouflage approached Alister. He pointed towards the road or the trail. Each group disappeared with his directive.

"You don't go on the mission?" Victor asked. Alister noted as activity increased, Victor moved closer.

"Not anymore," Allister said. Another man in a suit approached. Alister moved in the same direction as the man.

"Showtime," he said. "Victor, you should come too."

Victor followed the two to a white panel truck with no markings. They walked around the opposite side to find the panel removed and an awning attached to drown out the sun. Folding chairs sat in full view of many screens, each with a picture of a similar forest.

Victor leaned in to get a closer view of one, then turned back to the same picture behind him. He walked backward to get a look at the top of the van. A red dot blinked from above. On the screen, a shadow of his image broke in between the trees.

He took the seat beside Alister, who moved his chair over and back alongside Victor. Alister directed their attention to the two top screens. "Those two will carry the house in a few minutes," he explained. "The rest show the surrounding areas along with our perimeter."

"That's a lot of equipment," Victor noted.

"When there is unnecessary death involved, the allocations to solve the problem increase." Alister's explanation contained an almost philosophical twist.

"Too many deaths," Victor added.

A helicopter flew low over their heads. "Here we go," Alister rested his elbows on his knees as he leaned closer to the screens.

Harlot rushed into the guest bedroom. She threw her body at Salvi to knock him on his side. Surprised by her presence, he flung her off him as one would fling an ant off their arm.

"What the hell," Salvi yelled. He caught her arm as she took a swing at his head.

"You asshole," she barked back. She skittered over towards the nightstand to pull open the drawer. The top drawer contained sex gels and condoms, all scattered on the floor as the drawer crashed.

She pulled open the second. A small pistol fell into her hand. She brought the black steel up to meet Salvi's surprised face. "I loved you," she said, "while you werc with the FBI,"

"You knew?"

"Everybody knew, you idiot," she continued, "Yet I still loved you. I introduced you to the monkey twins, chemical geniuses, along with setting you up with Yarok and his people." Harlot rose up. "You made a mess of everything! This was supposed to be easy cash. No complications. But no, you couldn't do your part."

"Do my part? I am this operation! What did Yarok do?" Salvi paused. "Nothing! Yarok did nothing! He showed up at that place you stripped and…"

"And what? Set up distribution for the idiots in the lab." Harlot waved the gun in the air. "All you had to do was provide a place that they could cook. But no, you had to bring others in and start selling. What did you think that you could build a drug empire, and your daddy would respect you?"

Salvi's hand shot out to grab the barrel of the gun. Harlot tried to push him off with her foot, yet his body weight crashed into her legs. He pulled on the firearm to wrestle it from her hands.

Her foot came up to meet his cheek. The thump of something flying low froze both. "Shit," Salvi jumped out of reach. Loser appeared out of breath at the door.

"There's a—" Both reached the window in time to catch the shadow of a helicopter hover above.

"We got to run out of here," Salvi shouted.

"What about—" Loser pointed towards Harlot. Salvi trained the gun on the woman spread across his bed. He squeezed the trigger. Her eyes froze wide open as blood churned from her stomach.

"Let's go!" Salvi yelled as he waved the barrel towards the door. Loser mouthed, "I am sorry" in Harlot's direction. No words came back.

Behind the bathroom door, Alia slipped in and out of awareness. The thump outside the window echoed through her brain. She rested her head against the door, closed her eyes, and drank more toilet water in her mind.

Salvi ran down the long hall in the opposite direction of the stairway. From his perch behind the sheer drapes that covered a French door, he studied men covered in white suits entered his garage.

He went into the walk-in closet and reached up on the top shelf to remove a semi-automatic rifle along with a bump stock that he attempted to cram on top. He leaned the gun against the wall. On the other side of the closet, he located two more clips of ammunition.

Loser stood in the doorway.

"Grab the other gun," Salvi instructed. "We'll go out the back. You parked the Jeep in the woods?"

"What about the others?"

"What about them? Those idiots can do their monkey talk—"

"I met Yarok. He's going to be pissed."

"Screw Yarok."

"Yeah, but he and Harlot—"

"Loser, I am out of here. Follow me. Don't. I don't give a rats ass." Salvi pushed passed Loser. He went through a door in the sidewall, behind the bed. He disappeared from view.

Loser considered his options. The tube he slipped out of the lab leaned into his body. The Loser had an idea.

Johnny moved towards the house as the Haz-mat guys flushed out two men in border shorts and aprons. Both spoke in a foreign language, yet they kept their hands in the air as they chattered.

"Russian," Johnny heard one of his team say as they made their way up to the entrance.

He turned back towards his team. "We split inside. Go through each room carefully. Watch out for explosives when opening doors. The medics will start down the road on my signal. Ready." Johnny switched his two-way to the on position and said, "Go."

Loser had moved halfway down the staircase as the door slammed open. From his perch in the entryway, he saw others climb through the back gate.

Johnny surveyed the room. He stopped, surprised the Loser stood in plain view. On the one hand, he balanced a small gun. In his left held raised up in the air, the Loser grasped onto a small vile.

Johnny held up his hand. The two men behind him froze.

"Loser—" he began.

"What the freak are you doing here, DeLuca?" He walked down two more stairs. "I thought you retired."

"And I thought you worked for your brother."

"I guess we both were wrong," Loser moved down another stair. His eyes moved between Johnny and the front door. He heard a Jeep start-up reverb off the backside of the house, near the pool.

"Whatcha got there?" Johnny chin nodded towards the vile.

"Death in a tube," Loser cried. "Seriously, I drop this..." The laughter started up again. This time louder, it echoed against the stone. Loser now stood on the same level as Johnny. He moved around the parameter in the direction of the front door.

"Loser, there are people out front too," Johnny said. His voice calm and steady. "Let me help you." He waited for a response. When none came, he added, "For old times."

"Old times!" Loser screamed. "Old times! What old times? Think about it, DeLuca, you can't even remember my real name. Old times, seriously?" Loser made a move towards the door.

"Okay, okay. I can appreciate the point. But Lester, you never corrected me or anyone else. Yes, Lou and I played on the same sports teams in high school, and he introduced you as—"

"—my loser brother—"

"Exactly! Why didn't you correct me sooner—"

"—doesn't matter anyway," Loser now stood at the front door. He tucked the gun in his waistband to rest his left hand on the doorknob. His right still gripped the vile. "I'm going to leave now."

He pulled open the door. His body froze. Above his right eye, a trickle of red ran down his face. One of the men dived to catch the vile as Loser crumpled to the ground.

"Nice catch," Johnny said. "Please deliver that outside to the lab, and for God's sake, be careful." He turned his attention back to man piled on the ground. "Not the way you were supposed to go," Johnny whispered. He said a short prayer as the medics arrived.

One young man turned his head out the door to vomit on the front steps. The other connected a pulse monitor. "This doesn't look…" he said. The medic pulled the pulse monitor off. "I'm sorry."

"So am I," Johnny pressed the talk button on his two way. "Could you repeat that, please?" The person on the other end said a drone had picked up a Jeep driving in the opposite direction down the Salem trail. "And where does that trail go?"

"Salem, sir," the voice replied. Johnny was at number seven out of ten when another voice interrupted. "Mr. Deluca, the trail ends on Connecticut route 85."

"Thank you. Please put a block on the end. I want to do a quick search of the house, and then I will go there."

L.M. Pampuro

"Roger."

Johnny kicked open the first door to find Harlot Grace spread out across a king-sized bed. A pool of red shined below her breasts. Johnny reached out to place two fingers against her neck. A slight pulse greeted him.

"We need a medic up here," he shouted. Boots banged against the stairs behind him. Harlot fluttered her eyes open yet did not speak. "Hang in there, Gracie," Johnny encouraged. "The A-team is coming to fix you."

Her lips curved into the slightest smile as her eyelids closed. Johnny noted that even pre-death, Harlot Grace appeared as a sex kitten. He slapped the side of his head as the medics plowed passed.

"Your buddy downstairs is gone," the first one reported as he hooked up the same pulse monitor. He reached for Harlot's finger to attach the device. "This one has a shot." He pulled back the blanket. The wound appeared in her stomach region. The young man shouted orders. "You probably want to leave," he said as he stuck his hand into the flesh.

Harlot gurgled as he disappeared around the corner. The next two rooms appeared vacant. "Give both of those a quick search," Johnny ordered as he walked around the grand space. He pulled his phone out.

"Status!" Alister yelled on the other end.

"Lou's brother was shot and killed by one of our snipers," his voice became a monotone. "Harlot Grace is under medic care. She has a gunshot to the stomach area. At this time, we are not sure who shot her."

"What about Alia?"

"Whereabouts unknown. We are still looking."

"Look harder," Alister said. "We have a block on the connector road to route 85 along with a ground team in the woods. Two men, both Russian descent or at least that is the language they are speaking, were arrested outside the garage on the property, which was a drug lab."

Johnny continued to move room to room as Alister gave an overview of the situation. From Alister's public standpoint, they completed the primary mission goal of disabling the manufacturer and the drug facility. From his personal view, Alia is like a daughter to the old guy, and Johnny better find the P.I.T.A. quick.

Harlot's grace

Salvi jerked the wheel left and right as he attempted to avoid the random tree in the middle of his path. His gun slipped to the floor and bounced out at the last miss.

"Merda!" he yelled at the metal dropped into the greenery. "Io odio nature!" he exclaimed. His semi-automatic rifle rested on the passenger's seat. Salvi secured the machine with a quick tie of the seatbelt. The barrel position towards the floor shifted with the last bounce to rest near his right thigh.

Salvi pushed the object away with his right hand. A rut brought his grip back to the steering wheel and the gun against his leg. The trail veered off to the left, through a meadow of tall grass. Salvi went to the right. He kept his route along the pine tree-lined parameter.

Out of view, he heard the thump of a helicopter. His eye would catch a flash of a nearby drone, yet neither entered his sight. He took another hard left out of the pines at the end of the meadow. The trail split into red and green markings. He turned towards the green.

The terrain slanted upward and changed from dirt to rocks. The Jeep skipped from four to two tires. Salvi's knuckles turned white as he gripped the wheel tighter. The Jeep came back to all fours with a thud. Salvi swore.

The engine made a loud howl. The Jeep silenced as it reached the top. Salvi jumped out. From his direct view, Long Island Sound glittered in the distance. The water sparkled under the glow of sunshine. Salvi let out a deep sigh. "Nature not so bad," he said.

A drone buzzed in the woods behind him. He untied the shotgun, grabbed an extra clip from the floor, and shoved it in his jacket pocket. The strap dug into his shoulder. Salvi followed the ridge away from where he started. His Italian loafers did not provide the support his feet needed for a hike. Every few feet, his ankle twisted in an unnatural direction.

Low swear words in both English and Italian escaped from his lips as he attempted to balance on the loose rocks. The path markings faded. The gun weight increased with each step. His hands battled with mosquitos, green heads, and other parasites. His eyes deceived what lay beyond the trees.

The faint smell of marijuana drifted passed. He tried unsuccessfully to follow the scent. The green of the forest began to darken. Salvi's heart rate increased with the thought of sleeping in a forest. He jumped and raised the gun as a small animal ran across his path.

His finger rested on the trigger for a moment. He sat on a rock off to the side. Marijuana trickled in his nose again. A young lady's laughter, along with several others, filled the space. He moved the gun out of view as a group of teenagers in bright tie-dyed shirts walked along a trail, not even ten feet away.

"Hey now," one called out and gave Salvi a wave. He waved back—their move amongst the trees familiar.

He waited until he could barely see the last person before he began to follow. The trail of hard-packed dirt made it much easier to move. In the distance, a car engine turned over.

Salvi smiled. His day got better.

Alia pushed up on both wrists to force her body to lean over the side of the tub. The room spun less when she focused on the unattractive white surface. She straightened both arms to bring her body to a semi-standing position.

The room tilted to the right. Her arm hit the facet to turn on the cold water. From her waist, she dropped over the side of the tub. The cold water numbed her arm.

As Johnny walked to the main hall, he stuck his head in each room. Although different, each space featured the same layout. Bed, nightstand, table lamp, dresser, walk-in closet, and bath. The only place on the floor with something unique seemed to be the largest, in the end, assumed to be Salvi's.

He listened to the chatter on the radio at the same time his team comb through each room. Besides Harlot's blood, none had a clue of another human's presence.

At the top of the stairs, Johnny paused. On the two way, the news of Salvi's Jeep preceded a barrage of questions as to his unknown whereabouts. Johnny punched the wall with his left hand.

The pain ran up his arm. "Not the brightest move, sir," the uniformed state cop behind him monitored.

Johnny didn't comment. The cop opened his mouth again at the same moment Johnny asked, "Did you hear that?" The police shook his head no. Johnny pushed past him into the last room before the stairs. "Water. I hear the water."

"Behind that door," the cop drew his gun. He kicked the door hard. Nothing. He and Johnny kicked at the same time. Nothing. "Screw this," The cop aimed his gun at the lock. Johnny covered his ears, and both pulled back as the bullet shattered the lock to pieces.

The cop kicked open the door. Johnny grabbed Alia's head to move her sagging body out of the tub. He noted bite marks on one arm. She shivered at his touch.

"Medics!" Both yelled into their two ways and loud enough for their voices to echo throughout the house. Johnny carried her limp body onto the bed. Alia coughed.

"Hang in there, Al. We got the med staff on its way."

Her stoned eyes met Johnny's as she whispered, "Poison." She held up the arm with the bite marks. It dropped hard against the tub. A medic pushed Johnny out of the way. He cringed at the I.V. needle inserted into her arm.

As more medical staff arrived, Johnny found himself pushed back into the hallway. Alister stood off to the side. "How is she?"

"They say she'll be okay. Needs a stomach pump or something." Alister nodded. "You found the escape vehicle."

"Yes. Salvi is still on the loose."

"Where is Victor?"

"He left after we found the Jeep."

"Huh?"

"He went to tell Lou about his brother. I wanted to give the news in person. Victor has always worked with us."

"Huh," Johnny said. "Don't you worry about Salvi being his son?"

"I worry about Angelina's reaction. I worry about kids dropping dead for whatever they made here," Alister pointed at Johnny's chest, "Victor has no illusions about his middle child."

"If you say so." They moved back against the wall to allow a stretcher to pass. It disappeared into a room down the hall. A few minutes later, the medics maneuvered it back out, with a half-conscious Harlot on top. "She going to be okay?" Johnny asked as they passed.

"More or less," the medic answered.

"Loser's an idiot," Johnny said. "Harlot's an idiot, And Alia, she is the biggest idiot of them all!"

"Why is that?" Alister asked.

"Because she dated that *il asino*." Johnny turned to Alister. "I am going after him and then, no more." Alister let out a long sigh. "I mean it this time, Al. No contract jobs. No special favors. That one," he indicated the room and Alia, "is capable. Don't ever tell her I said that. Nana will be happy I am going to take Lucy away from here to someplace sane and making her more great-grandbabies."

Alister found amusement with the thought of Johnny surrounded by children. "But first—"

"But first I need to finish this." He moved his gun to his front waistband. "I am going to drive around and go on the other side."

"We have a team there."

"But I will find him."

Victor and Lou sat in their empty club. A bottle of Glenlivet Winchester along with two glasses between them on the table. A smoking Unbreakabowl in the ashtray next to Lou.

"Isn't this ours from when we sold the business booze?" Victor said as the label on the bottle came into focus.

"Yeah."

"Did we sell the business?"

Lou turned towards his lifelong friend. "No, Vic, we screwed the pooch." Both men cried. "To Lester the Loser," Lou raised his glass, "May my younger brother rest in peace."

"To Lester," Victor made the same gesture. "Salute."

"At least he is with mom and pops," Lou said.

"It's gonna get worst," Victor added.

"Isn't the phrase could be worst?"

"Yes, but thanks to my idiot son, the shit is going to hit that fan. Lou, I am worried. If Loser and Salvi were in business, who did they taint our club with?" He poured another drink for both. "I will have to tell my Angelina."

"God, help you with that one."

"No shit," Victor snickered. "I worry about her. And I worry about you."

"Me. Why?"

"Because neither of those two idiots is smart enough to put this together."

"Oh, crap."

"Oh, crap indeed." Victor held a lighter to the top of the Unbreakabowl. He sucked in the smoke before he handed it off to Lou. "When are we opening again?"

"I can have a crew in here tomorrow. The place is so wired that I can monitor," Lou caught his voice hitch. "We need a couple of Gino's boys to keep guard."

"Gino doesn't do drugs."

"Neither do we. That's why we need a little extra muscle."

Alister informed the governor that they had found and dismantled the drug lab that manufactured the tainted batch. On one monitor, he scrutinized the local news set up for the announcement. The rest contained dark pictures of the surrounding woods and Connecticut route 85.

L.M. Pampuro

Johnny arrived at the commuter lot as the sky turned pink and purple. On the opposite end, he studied a group of teenagers as they unloaded several cases of beer along with blankets.

They disappeared into the woods.

He parked his car about halfway into the lot, off in the already made shadows. More teenagers arrived and disappeared into the trees. Johnny turned on the GPS on his phone and waited. Alister's confirmation text came a moment later.

He walked towards the path. The woods echoed in laughter along with whiffs of skunk that Johnny concluded to be the top shelf Jamaican marijuana he used to pick up in Hartford's north end. He paused every couple of steps on the well-worn dirt trail to listen. Crickets, Beepers, and teenage girl giggles whispered around the tall pines.

A sudden burst of silence followed by awkward, "How ya doin's" sent Johnny into the shadows. He made his way back to the lot at the same moment headlights blinded his view.

A boy, no older than seventeen, jumped out of a beat-up shiny blue extended cab pick-up truck. He wrestled open the tailgate to grab a case of Bud Light along with a packed backpack.

The kid whistled as he arranged the backpack over one shoulder while he balanced the case on one knee while he tried to shut the tailgate. The kid jumped as Johnny slammed the gate from the opposite side.

"Thanks, dude," he said.

"I need a favor," Johnny began as the kid held out the case. Johnny waved him off. "No, not that. I need to hide in your truck."

"Hide. In. My. Truck?" the kid hesitated.

"Yeah, I'll give you," Johnny reached in his pocket and presented a hundred-dollar bill. "See my friend. He's coming down the path now. He thinks he's a military guy, anyway, his brain," Johnny twirled his finger by his ear. "He has a gun, not real, but he's going to try to take your truck—"

"Take my truck? Did Lisa put you up to this? Oh my god! My girl hates my truck and pulls these pranks," he considers the hundred.

"Yeah, I'm a friend of her dad—"

"Of course, you are," he laughs, "And the other guy too. Oh, I am going to get her back."

"I'm sure you are." Johnny tucked the hundred in the kid's front pocket before he opened the door. He crammed his body in the back seat. "Don't give it away, okay?"

"No problem. I thought you were going to take my brew." The kid turned towards the path yet gave Johnny a thumbs up as he shut the door. Johnny pushed open the back window.

"This your truck," Salvi's voice cut into the night.

"Yes, sir."

"Why you wink at me?" Johnny shook his head. He took out his sidearm and placed it on the floor near his right foot.

"I'm not, sir." The kid stared at the automatic rifle that now aimed at him. "That thing real?"

"Give me your keys?" Salvi instructed. "And which one of these domestics are yours?" The kid gestured to the truck. "Well?"

He reached into his front pocket to remove the keys, yet the uncooperative case of beer would not balance on his knee. The kid fidgeted for a moment. He extended the case into Salvi's arms.

"Thanks, bud," the kid said. He added, "Help yourself to a brewski." Salvi sneered at the canned beer with disgust.

"No, thank you," he said as he thrust the case back into the kid's arms. He grabbed the keys, pushed the kid aside, and yanked open the door. "Your friends went that way," Salvi steered towards the trail as he threw the gun over the center console to rest barrel down on the passenger's seat floor.

The kid waited. "*Partire*!" Salvi shouted as he turned the key. He revved the engine, threw the truck in reverse, while gravel flew in all direction. The kid dropped the case and began to wave his hands in the air as he chased the vehicle across the lot.

Salvi ran the stop sign at the exit to screech on to route 85. Johnny curved his fingers around the metal handle of his gun. As Salvi slowed for a red light, Johnny placed the barrel against his temple.

Salvi's body tensed,

"Take a right here and pull over," he instructed.

"Vaffanculo!" Salvi responded as he hit the break hard. Johnny's forehead bounced off the headrest.

"You son of a—" Salvi reached for the gun, yet Johnny repositioned the barrel and squeezed. Salvi screamed in pain. His foot rested on the gas, the truck careered to the right and bounced into a pine tree.

Salvi's head hit the steering wheel. Still conscious, his hand went for the automatic rifle. Johnny moved to slap the gun away as Salvi squeezed hard.

The sound of metal piercing off metal filled the cab. A bullet ricocheted into Johnny's right arm, while another scratched Salvi's forehead. Johnny's tightened his grip to wrestle Salvi's finger from its grasp.

Red and blue lights of emergency vehicles flash behind. "This ain't over," Salvi said. "I am going to—"

"It is over for me," Johnny said. He leaned his head against the back window and waited.

Harlot's grace

Alia appeared woozy as she stood outside the ambulance with Alister. Johnny lay inside, his fiancé Lucy by his side. Although they spoke Italian, Alia could comprehend most of the conversation.

"They are going away," she said. Her head spun like the time she had the flu and took two pills instead of the one prescribed. She rambled until Alister agreed to take her. Her ambulance parked next to Johnny's.

Salvi lost his leg. He got airlifted to Hartford Hospital, along with several agents. They were told he would be able to stand trial in a couple of months. "If someone doesn't take him out first," Johnny had added.

L.M. Pampuro

"Now, you will go with the ambulance," Alister said. Alia didn't move. Alister waved at the EMT's in the back. Once he had their attention, he pointed towards Alia. "I am heading up to talk to Victor," he walked with her. "You will go to Yale and obtain a detox. I should see you in a couple of days."

"Do I have to move again?" Alia said.

"Probably, but we don't have that information as yet. Let me see what they are planning for the courts and where we fit." He squeezed her hand. "You did good, kid."

Alia's lips turned up in a goofy grin. Her head tilted to one side. As the naloxone came down the tube to slip in her veins, she packed her apartment in her head.

L.M. Pampuro

For me to get my thoughts on paper, it takes a community of folks who inspire, motivate, encourage, critique, and move me to write my stories.
I am humbled to have this incredibly honest group of humans as family, friends, and colleagues.
This book came to life because I attended a workshop at The Rutgers Writers' Conference. I am grateful to Dr. Mary Bly for sharing her expertise.
My Beta readers, Evelyn Pampuro and Robert Calegari came through for me again with story ideas and character name suggestions.
Encouragement (and swift kicks) were delivered by Terri Meigs and Renee Stevens at the perfect time.
Shayna B's By The Sea provide inspirational cinnamon iced tea along with the best vegan cookie dough bites on the planet.
To the love of my life, my hubz, who did the best thing for my writing. He let me discover this world by providing silent reassurance.
And finally, to my awe-inspiring readers, thank you for reading my stories.
Peace.

L.M. Pampuro

Here is a sneak peek at the next chapter
for Alia Price, *Harlot's fire*.
Will there be revenge or consequences?
Coming Soon

L.M. Pampuro

Harlot's grace

Alia Price sat in the 1930's green leather chair across from her boss, the illustrious Alister Otis Reed.

Impressive in his mind, at least. Hands folded on her lap, her black LL Bean flats connected to the floor, back straight, without expression she watched Alister type vigorously into his computer. Each tap echoed in the paneled wood cavern. "We have a problem," his hands stopped moving as his eyes met hers, "the mob is after you."

Alia's laughter bounced out of the room. "After me? Whatever for? I didn't shoot Salvi!" Her laughter spilled into the hallway. Alister narrowed his eyes. Alia ran her hands over her face, sat up even straighter, then brought her hands back to her lap. Her shoulders started to shake. Alister took a long inhale off the lit cigarette before he placed the burning embers back to smolder in the ashtray. The building had been nonsmoking since before Alia's arrival, yet Alister didn't think the rule applied to him.

L.M. Pampuro

If anyone dared to complain to human resources, they got his standard answer "this is not a kindergarten class." However, on some days, Alia wondered.

"I'm not joking," he took another long inhale. "Salvi doesn't have the right background for this mob."

"I don't understand," Alia started to fidget in her chair. Her legs bounced below her. "No one knew about my assignment except," her eyes opened wide, "the people on the case with me. Alister?"

"I don't know."

"DeLuca?"

"Definitely not."

"Someone here?"

"Possibly," Alister snubbed out what remained of his cigarette in the overflowing ashtray. A few ashes escaped onto his desk. "Probably. I haven't got to there yet."

"Haven't got there yet?" Alia repeated. She twisted in her chair. "How far have you gotten?" She waited for a silent beat before she continued, "Really, Alister. I have been drugged, detoxed, and debriefed. What the heck do I do now? Go undercover? I have bills to pay and a life I might add."

Alister diverted his gaze. He shuffled a few papers on his desk and moved his body to take up the space of his executive chair.

"What are you not telling me?"

"Harlot Grace disappeared from the hospital."

Harlot Grace, the former stripper, somehow got connected with her ex. Alia's gut told her Harlot is involved in their current case. Why else would a gunshot victim leave a medical facility? She bit the inside of her cheek. "How did Harlot Grace disappear?"

"We don't know. She apparently walked out."

"Could Salvi have helped her?" Her ex kidnapped and drugged Alia along with other travesties; to move Harlot would be less complicated for him than ordering at Starbucks.

Alister moved a few more papers on his desk. He surveyed one with the state seal on the top with care. "The trial is scheduled for the end of the month."

"Alister," Alia cleared her voice. "How does the FBI lose a person?"

Alister gave his employee the stare across his desk. He spoke as if she hadn't. "Alia, I need you to do me a favor. Might you consider a little vacation?"

"Vacation or disappear?"

"Both. Mostly the latter."

L.M. Pampuro

"Is this one of those practical vacation situations where the company will cover my expenses? Like the last time?" She crossed her arms and legs to still her body. Alister reached for another cigarette, which he held between his tobacco-stained fingers. He pushed a piece of paper across the desk with his free hand.

"What's this?"

"Read it and find out." Alia took the offending document in her left hand, held out just enough to read the type. A bunch of cities is listed under the heading *The Flying Monkeys.*

"I don't understand." Alia brought the document closer. "What the hell is a flying monkey. Is this the list of sightings?" She laughed at her own joke. Alister's expression didn't change.

"Al, you are one of the best at digging up people's secrets."

"Thank you. I believe that is why you hired me."

"You have a gift that allows people to trust you, a great attribute in our line of work, however your attitude," Alia re-crossed her arms and legs in the opposite direction, "is probably going to get you killed someday."

The Howard Miller Schoolhouse clock to her left beat one loud tick at a time. Behind her co-workers laughed, gossiped, and took on the days growing list of the unthinkable. Without thought, her top leg began to bounce to the clock. Alister's typing brought in a second rhythm, one that matched up perfectly with the other sounds before it drifted apart into the chaos in the room.

"I think you should leave town until after the trial. You don't need to testify as we have people to represent your findings," Alia opened her mouth to speak yet Alister kept on going, "This here is a band of musicians who have got a lot of threats lately. Most have been online, yet last week someone threw a bottle filled with explosives at their tour bus. The bus was empty at the time, and no one got hurt but the chemical combination of nitro-methane with ammonium nitrate-- "

"Says whoever is responsible, they knew what they were doing." Alister shook his head. "Are there any buzzes about a motive?"

"That is exactly what we are looking for. The Monkeys have a following who enjoy a lot of weed with a bit of alcohol. Mostly a pretty mellow group..."

"What are you not telling me?" Alister sat back in his chair to admire his protégée. With only two years on the job,

Alia picked up on situations faster than most of his veterans. "I am going to find out anyway so you might as well—"

"Attorney Curry's son is their guitar player."

"Attorney General Curry of the great state of Connecticut?"

"One and the same. The same guy who is prosecuting your friends on the drug manufacturing charges—"

"Holy shit!"

"Alia!"

"Whoops. Sorry. I mean, oh my gosh! Curry's son is a rock star?" Alister started to smile as Alia took out a pen from her bag. She immediately began scribbling notes on the once offensive paper. "Why isn't Curry's office handling the explosive investigation?"

"Good question that I don't have an answer for. My theory is they believe the incident is tied to his present case. How would you like to be a groupie for a few weeks?"

"Groupie? Seriously? What is my cover going to be, tour slut?" She folded her body in half to lean one arm on the desk while resting her head in her hand. Alia mouthed specific phrases, underlined others, and placed question marks all around the page. "The report reads as if it is a slam-dunk that the drug mob is after the kid."

Alister knew better than to speak. She pushed the chair back to stand, the file still in her left hand, pen poised in her right. "What else is Curry involved in?" Alister just watched it. "Let's look beyond the case that involves me."

"Why?"

"That case is too easy." She flipped over to the last page to start to read backward. An old college trick to edit, she concentrated on every word, circling to add questions. The pen tapped against her front teeth incorporated the clock's tempo.

"You are wearing out my rug." Alia stopped to glare at her boss. "By all means, continue," he gestured in her direction.

"I have questions," she said.

"You are a journalist," he kept his face neutral. "You will have full access to all areas wherever they play. You are taking Miranda Silver's place as she is going undercover amongst the fans to try and shake out whoever is making the threats."

"She is looking for the mad bomber?"

"She is looking for the mad bomber." Alister pushed another file across the desk.

Alia reached across Alister's desk to grab a new pen out of the BOSS mug. She made a couple of notes on the file. "You want me to write a column?"

"About that. Miranda is doing some weekly articles under Miranda Stone. Write under her name, so people will think you are legitimate."

"I can't write under my name."

"You know you are not really a writer, right?"

"Yeah. But..."

Alister brought the unlit cigarette to his mouth to take a drag before opening every drawer of his desk. "Polly!" he screamed.

"We have a non-smoking office," came back from the hallway.

"Am I in charge?" Alister directed the question to Alia. She shrugged in return, "You do what you need to keep the illusion going. Make sure nothing happens to the kid and, in a few weeks, come back to a new assignment. Try to avoid getting kidnapped by hippies."

"Is the mob really after me?" Alia gave a half-smile.

Alister blew out a breath. "Alia, someone is making threats and noise. You uncovered one too many secrets. Harlot's disappearance adds to all of this." Her eyes watered, "While you are out there, you may want to keep your eyes open for

Harlot or Yarok Yarokov. His photo is in the second file." Alister brushed a few pieces of ash off his tie. "You are a good investigator, yet more importantly, you are an exceptional person. Could you just..."

"Fine. I will tour with The Flying Freakin' Monkeys, but let me warn you," she pointed her finger at Alister, "If I find out who gave me away..."

"Not if I find out first. Miranda's at some festival in Pennsylvania, the band is on the bill. She's expecting you tomorrow." Alister held up his cigarette, "and Alia, when you find these idiots, there is a team undercover at the fest. Don't be a hero - give the word."

"Are the others on my team listed in the file?"

"No. The situation dictates for you to just be if you understand." Alia nodded. "Know that you are surrounded by both those who will help you and—"

"—those who will kill me." Alia stood up, raised her hand to give a full salute.

"I'll make a call." Alister picked up his receiver. "Oh, and Al, I need your current laptop. You can pick-up another one downstairs before you leave."

"No problem." Alia walked across the office to her now former desk. An empty cardboard box sat on one side with a note attached: for personal items. Her desk contained no trinkets, no family photos, zero *Go Away* signs. In the corner hung one old Calvin and Hobbs cartoon. *You know, Hobbes, some days even my lucky rocketship underpants don't help.*[1] She reached out to remove the comic with care. "You are so right, Calvin."

Her computer bag lay on the chair out of sight, under her desk. One pull on the strap, a few clunks to her shoulder. Back in Alister's office, she placed the bag on the empty green leather chair. "I don't need the box." Alister handed her a piece of paper.

"One more thing, all updates go directly to me. Do not have Miranda send anything in and do not speak to anyone else in the office." She nodded. "Stay safe." Alia walked out of Alister's office back towards the common area. She stopped shy of the doorway.

People typed away as they stared at bright-lit screens. Heads cocked to the side, phone resting in between ear and shoulder. Others stood in groups pointing, making hushed comments. All pretended to be someone other than themselves. Her eyes scanned the entire room. Amongst the group of people, someone broke the

---

[1] Bill Watterson Calvin and Hobbs quotes

code. Someone gave up her identity. Right now, they could be in her presence.

"I heard Alister fired her this morning," came out of the employee lounge. The gossip already started. Part of her wanted to listen, maybe get a clue about who betrayed her. Her practical Virgo side forced her away, straight through the lobby. She slammed the bar that opened the door with both hands. Sunlight outlined her shadow. She walked across the dusty employee parking lot, turning back towards the massive brick building.

"This isn't over," she mumbled while shaking her fists. Alia got into her Outback and drove towards Pennsylvania. She was now a music journalist. Her mind assumed the identity necessary to complete the job.

L.M. Pampuro

Harlot's fire
Coming Soon

Get Social to Stay Updated:
Facebook.com/LMPampuro
Instagram.com/LMPampuro
Pampuro.com